Anonymous

Curiosities of Entomology

Anatiposi

Anonymous

Curiosities of Entomology

Reprint of the original, first published in 1871.

1st Edition 2023 | ISBN: 978-3-38212-631-5

Anatiposi Verlag is an imprint of Outlook Verlagsgesellschaft mbH.

Verlag (Publisher): Outlook Verlag GmbH, Zeilweg 44, 60439 Frankfurt, Deutschland
Vertretungsberechtigt (Authorized to represent): E. Roepke, Zeilweg 44, 60439 Frankfurt, Deutschland
Druck (Print): Books on Demand GmbH, In de Tarpen 42, 22848 Norderstedt, Deutschland

CURIOSITIES

OF

ENTOMOLOGY.

With Beautifully-Coloured Illustrations,

FROM DRAWINGS BY EMINENT ARTISTS.

LONDON:
GROOMBRIDGE AND SONS,
5, PATERNOSTER ROW.

CONTENTS.

BEES AND THEIR COUNTERFEITS.

1. Xylocopa nigrita, (male.)
2. Xylocopa nigrita, (female.)
3. Euglossa dimidiata.
4. Chrysantheda frontalis.
5. Euglossa cordata.
6. Anthophora elegans

CURIOSITIES OF ENTOMOLOGY.

BEES AND THEIR COUNTERFEITS.

THE Bee is a name common to all the species of a very numerous tribe of Insects of the order *Hymenoptera*. The bee family was termed by the great French naturalist Latreille, *Mellifera* (honey-gatherers), or *Anthophila* (flower-lovers), both terms being characteristic of the general habits of the family, but the former the most appropriate. In England alone about 250 species have been discovered. No insect is so well known to the general public as the common hive-bee (*Apis mellifica*) of North-Western Europe. All the habits, peculiarities, and wonderful and interesting social arrangements of this insect have been described and explained in numerous works; but, although the natural history of our common hive-bee has been made so generally known, the other members of the bee family have found but few popular historians, and less is generally known about them, except to entomologists, than about other far less interesting insect families.

Yet there are many wonderful peculiarities connected with different species of the bee tribe which would amply repay the labour of a little observation and study. We shall, therefore, direct the reader's attention to a few remarkable species of British and foreign bees, more especially with reference to certain extraordinary resemblances which exist between some of the honey-collecting species and those belonging to the parasitic or cuckoo class, which will lead to the notice of still more curious resemblances that exist between bees and certain insects belonging to the distinct order *Diptera*. These last, though only furnished with two wings, while the bees and the whole order (*Hymenoptera*) to which they belong have four, yet bear such a striking resemblance to the bees, in company with which they are found, that an untrained observer would not, certainly at a first glance, perceive the difference that really exists.

One of the most remarkable features in those species of bees which live in societies, as is well known in the case of the common hive-bee, is the existence of a third sex, the neuter or worker; and there are other singular peculiarities of this sort in less known species, such as the existence of two distinct kinds of females.

The material of which the egg-cells are composed is very various in the different species. The comb of the hive-bee, as is well known, is made of wax, secreted in a peculiar manner;* but other species, though forming a comb almost identical in appearance, make it by the manipulation of certain substances which they reduce to a material resembling common paper; while others form cells of sand, moistened with a glutinous secretion, which reduces it to a kind of tenacious cement.

Some of these species, again, collect an inferior kind of honey, while others only collect pollen, of which they place a small mass or ball in each cell in which an egg is to be deposited, so as to furnish a supply of food for the grub or larva to subsist on till full grown. This substance is collected solely to form food for the larvæ. The exact quantity sufficient is prepared by the instinct of the parent; and, in fact, when that is consumed, the young grub bee is compelled to subside at once into the torpor during which his change of organisation is to take place, as he has no powers of locomotion, being

* For a description of the process, and for all general information respecting the habits and management of the common hive-bee, see "The Beekeeper's Manual," by Henry Taylor. Price 4*s*. Groombridge & Sons, 5, Paternoster Row, London.

a clumsy maggot-formed larva, and, being placed at the bottom of a smooth-sided cell, has no means of seeking food for himself.

In many instances it is only by the bees travelling from flower to flower that the pollen or farina is carried from the male to the female flowers, without which they would not fructify. One species of bee would not be sufficient to fructify all the various sorts of flowers, were the bees of that species ever so numerous, for it requires species of different sizes and different constructions. "M. Sprengel found, that not only are insects indispensable in fructifying different species of *Iris*, but that some of them, as *I. xiphium*, require the agency of the larger humble-bees, which alone are strong enough to force their way beneath the stilé flag; and hence, as these insects are not so common as many others, this *Iris* is often barren, or bears imperfect seeds."

The tribes of parasitic bees which do not make cells to contain honey or pollen for the separate use of each infant bee, visit the nests of their more industrious cousins, and surreptitiously place an egg of their own in the cell containing the honey or pollen, as the case may be.

"It was formerly believed," says Mr. Noel Humphreys, "that the egg of the parasitic bee was placed in the same cell with the egg of the honey-bee, and that being hatched first, the young parasite devoured all the food, leaving the infant of the honey-bee to find himself born to an empty larder, and consequently speedy starvation; but more recent observation has led to the conclusion that this is not the case, but that the parasitic bee, on entering the nest, selects cells already furnished with honey or pollen, but in which no egg has yet been laid. While the unsuspicious female proprietors of the nest, finding an unexpected egg deposited in the cell they first visit, exhibit no sign of surprise, but pass on to the next, not seeming to be at all disturbed by the presence of the uninvited deposit; just as small birds make no attempt to exclude the egg of the cuckoo, but hatch it, and rear the young intruder along with their own offspring. This occurs in the nests of wild bees constructed in different situations, some kinds making an excavation expressly, others adopting the deserted work of some other insect, or taking advantage of an accidental hollow. For instance, *Anthidium manicatum*, one of our summer bees, generally uses the holes bored in willow stumps by the *Cossus ligniperda;* but a nest of this species was once found, as described by Mr. F. Smith, in the key-hole of a garden door. Some of the humble-bees, on the other hand, carefully construct their own burrow. A beautiful exotic species, a large and powerful bee, has received the specific name of *Latipes*, from the singular broadening and strengthening of the front pair of feet. These broadened feet assume somewhat of the character of the front feet of the mole, or rather those of that curious insect, the mole cricket. These enlarged feet, with the thick brushes of strong hairs with which they are furnished, are evidently excavating implements, and no doubt the works produced by their agency are of a very interesting kind; but entomological discovery has not at present made us acquainted with the nest architecture of this handsome insect. A pretty little English bee, one of the solitary kind, often makes its burrow in sheltered parts of hard gravel walks; an affair evidently of very great labour, as the female bee, who is the sole architect in this instance, frequently comes to the opening of the burrow to rest, when the male companion commences flying rapidly round and round his mate, as though to encourage her to renew her task."

Among those species most subject to parasitic intruders is the common garden humble-bee, *Bombus hortorum*, of which we give an engraving (Fig. 1) side by side with its parasite *Apathus barbutellus* (Fig. 2). These bees so closely resemble each other, that one may easily be mistaken for the other, even by those aware of the resemblance, till after a close examination, as they are almost identical in colour, size, and general form. There is, however, one marked difference, which is easily perceived when the eye has been taught where to look for it; for the hind legs of the honey or pollen collector invariably have an enlarged tibia, or large bone of the leg, the flattened and somewhat hollowed breadth of which serves as a receptacle in which the pollen collected from flowers is carried to the nest. This peculiarity of form is seen in the engraving, Fig. 1; while the corresponding part of the hind leg, as shown in Fig. 2, will be observed to be simply rounded. These parasites, having neither the instinct to collect food for their expected progeny, nor, in fact, the means of carrying it home, even if they had the desire, have been considered by naturalists to be entirely without those parental and home instincts which distinguish the collecting and harvesting kinds, and from this apparent apathy in regard to providing food or protection for their young being the chief charac-

1 2 3

teristics of all parasites, the whole genus has been named *Apathus*, by an eminent English naturalist, in place of the name *Cuculinæ*, or cuckoo-bees, given to them by Latreille. The light band on the thorax, or forepart near the head, is less distinct in the *Apathus*, and the abdomen is less profusely furred.

The insect shown in Fig. 3 is still more curious, and although, at first sight, it seems to resemble both the bees so much as to be mistaken for them, it will be found on closer examination to be not only far from identical, but radically different. It is, in fact, merely the size and general colouring which deceive the untrained eye. On examination, almost every part of its structure will be found to be very distinct from that of the bee: the eyes are differently placed, and differently formed, while their size and colour are nearly identical with those of the bees; the antennæ, instead of being horny and robust, like those of the bee, are delicately slender and feathered, like some kinds of moths; but these, not being conspicuous appendages, escape the attention of the ordinary observer. The thorax is, however, furred with orange hairs next to the head, which become yellow near to the abdomen, leaving the centre of the thorax black; the segments of the abdomen nearest the thorax are clothed with yellow fur; the central segments are black, and the last segments, or tail, are white. This is precisely the colouring of both the bees shown in Figs. 1 and 2; but then the single pair of wings shows the trained observer that it belongs to another and distinct order of insects, the *Diptera*, or two-winged order. The legs, also, have not the enlarged or honey-bearing tibiæ, and even the anatomical structure of the body itself, though disguised by the fur clothing of the identical colour of that of the two bees, is of itself amply sufficient to show that the insect belongs to another and very distinct class.

"Still," says Mr. Noel Humphreys, "the close general resemblance of this insect, *Volucella plumata*, is indisputable, and as it passes into the nest of the bee, in order to deposit its eggs (one to each) on many of the living larvæ of the bees, it might certainly, to a casual observer, pass for one of the family, while entering the bees' nest on its mission of murder to the infant bees in their cell-cradles. The egg of this parasite being deposited in the warm folds of the soft skin of the bee-larva is rapidly hatched, and it at once proceeds to its unnatural feast, slowly devouring the foster parent whose breast had warmed it into life; the bee larva being a soft, legless grub, with no powers of escape, very closely resembling that of the humble-bee, and indeed of the hive-bee also. The larva of the *Volucella*, with its broad tail, armed with sharp spines, and its muscular body tapering to the head, and furnished with rigid serrations along each side, forms a striking contrast to the soft, helpless larva of the bee. Like all the larvæ of the *Syrphidæ*, to which the genus *Volucella* belongs, it is blind; but, resting attached by the broad tail, it moves its head rapidly about as a feeler, before changing its position. The spikes at the tail may be adapted to enable it to raise itself up the smooth sides of the cell of the bee larva, in case that one infant bee should prove insufficient, and that it might require to pass on to the next cradle. But it may be as well to describe the progress of the parasitic larva on the supposition that one baby bee will prove enough for its purpose. The devoted larva of the bee, then, is gradually eaten alive by the parasite; which, with seemingly horrible instinct, spares all the actually vital parts, taking only the more fleshy portions, until the carnivorous young *Volucella* feels itself full fed and ready to undergo its torpid state of change. Then, the last remains of the wretched infant bee are greedily consumed, and the parasite passes into its sleepy chrysaline stage, taking its long *siesta* in the comfortable cradle whose infant tenant it has devoured, and from which it eventually comes boldly forth in all the pride of its winged and perfect state, walking out of the bee home as from its own proper abode, and attracting no notice whatever from the bees, in whose nursery it has performed the odious task of eating a baby bee, and appropriating its comfortable cradle cell. The stolid unconsciousness with which the bees allow this insect vampire to pass out and escape from the scene of his horrid proceedings with impunity, has induced some naturalists to believe that the carnivorous *Volucella* owes its safety to its complete disguise in the colouring of the bee, which is supposed to be so perfect as to deceive the bees themselves into the belief that these strangers are members of their own fraternity. Messrs. Kirby and Spence observe, 'did these intruders venture themselves among humble-bees in a less kindred form, their lives would probably pay the forfeit of their presumption.' This statement, however, though appearing so plausible, is not borne out by analogy, there being many parasites on bees which do not bear the slightest resemblance to the insects whose nests they invade. Not only are some of the *Diptera*, who deposit their eggs in the nests of bees, very unlike the bees whose homes they infest, but even the parasitic bees themselves do not always resemble the bees whose nests they appropriate. For instance, the species *Eucera longicornis* has a *broad* brownish body, without any conspicuous mark, while its parasitic relative, *Nomada sex-fasciata*, has the *narrow* body of a wasp, and, as its name implies, six conspicuous yellow bands on the abdomen, which, with the intermediate black spaces, make it a very distinct-looking creature indeed. In some of the exotic bees more especially, the distinct aspects of the harvesting bee and the parasite are very striking; they are, in fact, so much so, that the insects might be thought to belong to entirely different families. The beautiful Brazilian bee, *Euglossa dimidiata*, has an attendant parasite as totally unlike it as it is possible to conceive of insects of the same order. *Euglossa dimidiata* is one of the most beautifully and variously coloured of the whole bee tribe." The specimen from which our representation, No. 3 in the coloured plate of "Bees and their Counterfeits," facing the title-page, is taken, "was captured by Mr. Bates, at Para, in the Brazils; and it is found in other tropical parts of South America. Latreille described this handsome species in Schomberg's Fauna of British Guiana; but it had been previously described by Fabricius, from specimens taken at Cayenne, and named by him *Apis dimidiata;* subsequent divisions of the family having rendered another generic name necessary, this beautiful species was attached to the genus *Euglossa.* It forms its nest by boring tubular hollows in large reeds, and there is a specimen of a reed in the British Museum bored in this manner by this bee, or by a bee belonging to a closely allied genus. Into such a tube the parasite bee penetrates, for the purpose of depositing its egg in the cells which have been furnished with honey or pollen by *Euglossa dimidiata.*

"In this case, in order to support the theory of Messrs. Kirby and Spence, it would be more than usually necessary that the intruder should be furnished with a very complete disguise, as he must, in such a narrow tubular home, necessarily come to very close quarters with the master of the house. Yet, on the contrary, the whole aspect of the parasite of *Euglossa dimidiata* is not only extremely different, but its appearance is of that striking character calculated to excite immediate attention. Instead of being soft and furry after the fashion of the humble-bee tribe and their allies, he is entirely hard, smooth, and glittering—the entire body, thorax and abdomen, and also the legs, being of a light vivid metallic green, like that of our rose-beetle. It might be urged, on the other hand, that, although not provided with a security in the form of a disguise, a defence of another kind has been substituted, in the suit of impenetrable plate-armour, of magnificent green bronze, in which this insect is incased. But I feel convinced that it is entirely futile to attempt to explain the nature of providential arrangement, and point out the secret purposes for which either apparent analogies or discrepancies were devised. The best explanations offered, indeed, are too full of contradictions to be for a moment seriously accepted as revelations of intended purpose. As a ready example of the contradictions to which such speculations must be liable, I may mention here, that although the parasitic bee, which infests the nests of *Euglossa dimidiata*, is entirely unlike the harvesting-bee, whose home he invades, yet the doubly-unfortunate *Euglossa* has a second enemy, in the form of a gigantic *Diptera*, whose similarity to the bee is most curious. This enormous fly-bee, *Asilus fasciatus*, has, it is true, only two wings, but those being of deep brown to half their length, and transparent for the remainder, bear an extraordinary general resemblance to those of the bee; while the colouring of this handsome insect being nearly identical with those of the bee, and the size and shape of the markings being almost identical, the general resemblance becomes very remarkable; hence the conspicuous appearance of one enemy is rendered utterly useless as a defence, while the seemingly perfect disguise of another apparently favours his fatal entrance to the nest."

The handsome *Xylocopa nigrita* (Figs. 1 and 2 in the coloured plate of "Bees and their Counterfeits") is a native of Sierra Leone, and remarkable for the full deep velvety black of the greater part of the body, while the sides of the abdomen are conspicuously fringed, and partly covered, with milk-white furry hairs; the effect of which call to mind the appearance of an aged negro, of the same part of the African coast, whose woolly hair has become white with age. The legs, also, are thickly fringed on one side with a similar white fur, and the face is white, with large brown eyes. The wings are nearly opaque, and of deep dull purple, with a metallic gloss, bronzy-red towards the extremities. The *Diptera*, or two-winged counterpart of this insect (Fig. 5 in the coloured plate), "has all the characteristic contrasts of black and white, similarly disposed, even to the white face and brown eyes; while the opaque, iridescent wings are precisely similar in tone and colour. The somewhat longer legs, the single pair of wings, and the different structure of the antennæ, at once prove to the entomologist that these two insects are not only not the same, but that they belong even to different 'orders.' They are, however, in all probability, found together, like the other bees and *Diptera* which so strongly resemble each other—the larva of the *Diptera*, no doubt, preying upon the larva of the bee. In proof of this hypothesis, it may be stated that both specimens were brought to England from the west coast of Africa, the bee from Sierra Leone, the bee-fly from Port Natal, and probably both will eventually be found in the same district. The bee exhibits, in an unusual degree, a peculiarity common to many of the family, namely, a marked difference in the general aspect of the two sexes." The other exotic bees figured in the coloured plate are from South America.

Some of the most beautiful of the exotic bees are parasites and produce neither honey nor pollen; but it is probable that some of these may hereafter be found to have been incorrectly classed as parasites, and be proved to be honey collectors; for the absence of the large flattened hollow in the tibia or middle joint of the hind leg, which appears to be absolutely necessary to the honey carrier, is not proof positive of parasitism, for among *Andrenidæ*, the genus *Prosopis*, although without the usual apparatus for collecting honey, has nevertheless been recently proved to be a honey producer, filmy cells containing liquid honey having been found in its nest, which has been discovered formed of tubes in the main stem of the bramble; and that indefatigable entomological observer, Mr. F. Smith, the well-known author of the British Museum Catalogue of *Hymenoptera*, having watched a specimen of the genus *Sphecodes* of the sub-family *Acutilingues* while in the act of forming its burrow, discovered that it was a pollen producer, although without the usual organs for carrying the pollen.

"Some of the exotic bees," says Mr. Noel Humphreys, "are almost as richly coloured as the more gaudy butterfly tribe, and at the same time are of such conspicuous size as must render them very remarkable objects, winging their rapid and always musical passage among the exuberant vegetation of the tropics. A thoughtful spectator seeing for the first time in their native wilds these gigantic and magnificently tinted bees, robbing the nectaries of tropic flowers of sweets whose mere perfume seems almost too delicious, could scarcely forbear picturing to himself the produce of unknown kinds of honey, of a luscious sweetness and exquisite flavour, as yet undreamed of. If (he might reflect) those mean little plants of wild thyme, trailing their humble stems among the scanty herbage of our bleak northern hills, can yield delicious honey to that poor little brown gatherer, the old hive-bee, what may one naturally expect to be the result of honey-gathering by such a noble race of bees as these of the tropics, and with such exquisite flowers to gather from! Such might easily be conceived to be the exclamation of an observer of the flight of bees among the gorgeous plants in one of the natural gardens of some intertropical valley; and he would think of those bees mentioned by Amer which make natural hives of the cavities of rocks, laying up honey in large pouches, or cells, of the size of a pigeon's egg, and which, being dark coloured, and hanging to the sides of the hive in clusters, look like bunches of delicious grapes, containing, in fact, a juice far more sweet. He might think also of what Clavigero, the Spanish historian of Mexico, says of a bee, evidently of a nearly allied species, which abounds in Yucatan, and produces the famous honey of Estabentiem, the finest in the world, which is said to be taken from the bees every two months. These bees are, however, small inconspicuous creatures, evidently belonging to the same group as our own honey hive-bee, though distinguished from it by being stingless. The most magnificent bees are, on the other hand, not of the true honey kind. They belong principally to the class of solitary bees, including a few of the humble-bee class and their relatives. These last, though it is true that many of them of the 'social' kinds do collect honey, yet manipulate it in a very inferior manner to that of the hive-bee. Other kinds only collect pollen, which, being exclusively intended as food for the young larvæ, is generally rolled into little balls or pills, one being placed in each of the cells in which an egg is to be deposited."

The truly magnificent insect, *Xylocopa nobilis* (Fig. 6) was captured by Mr. Wallis, in the island of Celebes, an almost unknown collecting ground, from which we may expect to obtain many other new and splendid additions to our cabinets of exotic insects. Its body is of the richest conceivable velvet black, with a rich brown bloom upon it; this deep ground colour being banded with transverse stripes of the richest gold colour, the two central stripes producing a peculiarly bright and sparkling effect from their extreme narrowness. The wings are semi-opaque, and their colour modulates from a deep indigo-violet in the centre to a rich bronzy green at the extremities, the violet becoming nearly crimson where the wings join the body.

A new species from India (No. 5, not yet named, in the second coloured plate) is perhaps even more beautiful; for though the usually slender and elongated body is entirely black, the wings exhibit the most gorgeous iridescent colours that can be imagined. They are of a reddish tawny bronze at the ends, getting redder towards the centre, where the red suddenly but softly blends into a rich metallic green, followed by a portion of rich deep blue, which in its turn becomes violet at the base of the wings.

Centris flavopicta (No. 1, in the second coloured plate) is one of the many fine insects brought from the banks of the river Amazon, and is so called from the subdued yellow tone of the abdomen and legs, the latter being finely painted or marked with dark brown.

Oxæa flavescens (Fig. 2) is a remarkably brilliant insect, to which no engraving or painting can do adequate justice. The abdomen is of metallic orange of the greatest richness, but entirely without gloss, striped across with bands of pale glittering yellow, which have the appearance of positive bands of the most highly burnished pale gold.

Euglossa analis (Fig. 3) is one of the pretty and gaily-coloured small bees of the Brazilian forests, which have often been described; but few of the more recently discovered species surpass this specimen in brilliant metallic tinting.

Euglossa Brullei (Fig. 8) is another species of the same genus.

Euglossa violacea (Fig. 7) is so well known that it would not have been included in our plate, but for the tempting contrast which its rich violet offered to the orange and yellow tones of the other specimens.

But the most beautiful as well as the largest of this genus, is the exquisite Brazilian insect *Euglossa pulchra* (Fig. 4), so named by Mr. F. Smith. The most highly finished engraving would do but scanty justice to its beauty. The colour of the face is rich metallic apple-green, contrasting finely with the ruddy brown of the large eyes. The thorax is of the finest velvety purple, appearing of a deep black in the parts which do not receive a direct light. The two upper segments of the abdomen are of a bright red-violet, inclining to crimson; the remaining segments being of a vivid metallic straw colour, resembling the colour of electrum, or gold paled by an admixture of silver, a natural combination anciently found in the sands of the celebrated river Pactolus, and from which some of the most ancient gold money of Sardis was coined.

BRITISH AND FOREIGN BEETLES.

THE term Beetle has frequently been used as the name common to the species of the family *Scarabæidæ*, but it is more commonly and properly used to designate those insects which are covered by a strong horny substance, the abdominal part of the body being protected by two sheaths under which the wings are folded. Hence the term is synonymous with *Coleoptera*. No form of animal life has attracted the attention of naturalists more constantly, and proved more generally instructive, than that of insects; and "among these," says Mr. Noel Humphreys, "the beetle tribe especially were noticed by the ancients at a very early period, from two very opposite points of view—superstition and philosophy. With the sacerdotal naturalists of Egypt, who had carefully observed the habits and transformations of the Beetle, that insect became a symbol of the principle of metempsychosis, and other theological dogmas; while with the Greeks, in the hands of Aristotle, it became an example of one of the acutest methods of classification, founded on anatomical structure, that science ever devised. Finding that the whole of the beetle family were furnished with wings protected by a sheath-like covering, he compounded of the word χολεος, a scabbard or case, and πτερά, wings—a term which is still generally applied by naturalists to the entomological order comprising the beetles. It is true that some of the insects included by Aristotle in his great family of Coleoptera, have been removed by modern science to other natural orders; but the great distinctive feature, as a class definition, and also the very name by which the father of natural history distinguished it, are both retained in the natural philosophy of modern

BRITISH BEETLES AND THEIR FOREIGN RELATIVES.

[illegible] Cicindela campestris.
3. [illegible]
4. [illegible]
[illegible]

5. Pachyrynchus speciosus.
6. Pachyrynchus reticulatus.
7. Eupholus Schönherri.
8. Carabus intricatus.

times, no better character or name having been found for the order of insects to which they were originally applied by the Macedonian entomologist of two and twenty centuries ago. More than one among our modern naturalists have sought to alter the venerable term invented by the founder of their science, but none of their suggestions have been permanently adopted."

During the winter months, when the more generally attractive classes of insects are but rarely to be met with, the entomologist may still seek with success for several kinds of beetles, which may be found under large loose stones, or beneath flakes of dead bark, or in the shelter of matted clumps of moss.

Our native beetles are not so conspicuous in their forms, or so finely coloured as those which attracted the attention of Aristotle in the fine climate of Greece; but there are many among them of considerable beauty, and in fact our native species of *Cicindelidæ* are not surpassed by their near relatives in the more southern parts of Europe, and are scarcely inferior in beauty to some of their intertropical cousins with which we shall compare them.

The commonest, and at the same time the prettiest, of the British species of *Cicindela*, is the well-known *C. campestris* (Fig. 6), an elegant and active little green beetle, with yellowish spots, that may be found in sandy districts on any fine sunny day of early spring. This species has long been known to collectors as the Tiger Beetle, being so named, as some say, from its spots and stripes; but as others assert, from its carnivorous nature, preying as it does upon other insects, and occasionally even upon its own species. They were also called "sparklers" by the old collectors, from their brilliant aspect when the sun shines upon them, especially during the short but rapid flight which they indulge in during sunshine, particularly when alarmed, when they make a humming noise like bees. M. Desmarets was the first to observe the method pursued by the larvæ of Tiger Beetles for capturing their prey. They construct, as he informs us, a narrow tunnel or pit of the depth of about eight or ten inches perpendicularly, sometimes more than a foot deep, according to the nature of the earth in which it is formed, which is generally sand. When complete, they climb to the mouth of the tunnel, making their broad flat head, which they cover with sand, form a kind of trap-door to this treacherous oubliette. They sustain themselves in the desired position by means of two hook-like appendages, till a small insect passes over the living trap-door concealed by a treacherous layer of sand, when the larva immediately allows itself to drop to the bottom of the burrow, followed of course by the tumbling victim, who is speedily devoured. If the insect passing over the trap is too large to fall readily into the tunnel, it is seized as it passes, and dragged forcibly down to its destruction in the dark pitfall. Nothing is known of the larvæ of exotic *Cicindelæ*, but Latreille considers that in all probability they resemble, both in form and habits, those of the European species. The female of *C. campestris* may be distinguished from the male by the presence of two additional buff spots. *C. Germanica* is another British species, and also *C. hybrida*, of which last there is a specimen in the collection of the Linnæan Society, with the name in the handwriting of Linnæus himself.

Cicindella Chinensis (Fig. 7), an exquisitely beautiful species, is one of the most common insects of the tea-growing districts, and is often found in chests of tea imported into this country. It is a curious fact that, while none of the tropical species materially surpass our own either in form or colour, this remarkably handsome insect, inhabiting a climate very similar in general temperature to our own, far exceeds our *C. campestris* both in size and beauty. Our representation will give a fair general idea of the beauty of this finest of the exotic *Cicindelidæ*, but no painting can perfectly imitate the richness and at the same time the extreme delicacy of its colouring. Exquisitely clouded markings of deep purple, rich in tone and texture as tinted velvet, form the chief feature of the colouring; these masses of purple shading off at the edges into the rich apple-green which forms the general ground, the green becoming in places nearly a silvery azure, and this green ground being again varied by conspicuous marks of delicate buff; the central ridges of the elytra being also of a buff tone, with a metallic gloss of gold.

Though exceedingly numerous, our native species of the extensive order *Curculionidæ* are all small and insignificant, while the exotic genera of this tribe contain many of the most splendid insects yet known. For instance, *Otiorhynchus ligustri* (Fig. 1), the common *Curculio* of the Privet, is of a dull olive brown colour, with the tuberculations of the elytra rather paler, and has no pretensions to beauty except perhaps its general elegance of form, while his foreign relatives are not only more than four times the size of our native kinds, but their splendour of colour often equals, if it does not surpass, that of the whole insect world. The *Eupholus Schönherrii* (Fig. 7) forms perhaps the most remarkable contrast among exotic species to our native *Curculios*, both in size and beauty. This magnificent insect was discovered in the island of Celebes, by the officers of "La Coquille," the French ship of discovery that circumnavigated the world in 1833. The first specimen of this then unknown relative of the *Curculios* was taken at a little seaport of Celebes, called Dory, one of the hottest parts of that intertropical region, and which, in the general account of the voyage, is described as swarming with resplendent insects of various kinds; and it was eventually placed in the collection of M. Chevrolat. M. Guerin, describing it for the zoological section of the voyage of "La Coquille," made it the type of a new genus, which he called Eupholus, from the Greek words *ευ*, fair, and *φολις*, a scale, in allusion to the powdery bloom, similar to the minute scales of the wings of butterflies, with which its elytra are covered; which term was adopted by Boisduval when he described other allied species discovered in the voyage of the "Astrolabe." The representation in the plate can give but a faint idea of this subdued metallic kind of lustrous bloom, but the general distribution of colour is well represented. M. Guerin describes the ground colour as being of a lovely glaucous green, slightly metallic, the corslet being brilliant azure, passing off imperceptibly to a delicate green at the edges; the wing-cases having transverse stripes of deep velvety black, and the space comprised between the first and second pair of stripes, and between the third and fourth, being a fine light blue. The specimen in the British Museum, sent from Celebes by our enterprising collector, Mr. Wallis, does not entirely agree in colour with M. Guerin's description. "This may be accounted for," says Mr. Noel Humphreys, "by the colours having changed or faded in dead specimens, or from the specimens in M. Chevrolat's collection, or the one in the Museum, being a variety. The colours of the large specimen in the British Museum, and also of several smaller specimens, are as follow:—The head, ochreous green, with deep brown stripe; the corslet, a brilliant lilac, becoming pink in high light, and changing to green towards the edges; the elytra are of a bluer lilac, and have five transverse bars of black, the spaces between the first and second bar and the third and fourth being a greenish white, which contrasts very delicately with the blue lilac of the other portions of the wing-cases; the legs are brilliant metallic green, with the exception of the joints, which are of a rich purplish azure and very brilliant; the antennæ are of a delicate cinereous green, with brown tips. I believe the largest specimen in the Museum is marked as a variety; but as there are several specimens exactly like it, except in size, our specimens may prove to be distinct species." Several other species of this new genus have since been discovered, some at the same port, Dory, and other parts of New Guinea, and the adjacent islands during the subsequent voyages of the "Astrolabe" and the "Zelee," all magnificent insects, with green and blue elytra finely striped with black bands, but all of inferior size and beauty to the original type of the genus, which, in its turn, is inferior to the variety or new species in the British Museum.

Another genus of exotic Curculionidæ, the species of which form a striking contrast with our native kinds, on account of their great brilliancy, is principally founded on the beautiful insects of this class from the Philippine Islands, which were procured a few years ago by Mr. Cuming, an English merchant residing at Lima, and trading from thence to the

Philippines: all of them were till then unknown to European naturalists. For the classification of these insects, M. Germar first established the genus *Pachyrhynchus*, formed of the Greek word παχος, thick, and ρυγχος, a beak or bill, from the thick elongation of the head, as distinct in character from that of the European *Otiorhynchus*. The new name was first given to a single species which was at that time commonly received from Manilla, being the only species then known. MM. Eydoux and Souleyet met with and described another species from the same place in 1839. But these were nothing to the wonderful collection of this glittering Curculian group brought to Europe by Mr. Cuming in 1840, which astonished the entomological world with their novelty and splendour. From among those purchased of Mr. Cuming by the trustees of the British Museum we have given three in our plate, namely, *P. gemmatus* (Fig. 4), *P. speciosus* (Fig. 5), and *P. reticulatus* (Fig. 6). *P. gemmatus* is by far the largest and most splendid; and, although sufficiently splendid to the unassisted eye, it is only in the microscope that all the magnificence of its details can be fully observed and appreciated; for its splendours are of that minute character which cannot be exhibited in a drawing unless greatly magnified, and even then the glitter of the metallic effects could not be pourtrayed. The ground colour is a rich crimson maroon, with a golden gloss in the high lights. But the large spots, which have the appearance of being inlaid with a variety of gems, form the chief feature. In the centre of each of these gemmed circlets the inlaid colours appear to be composed of minute triangles of turquoise and emeralds, with granules of silver between, while towards the margin the emerald disappears, and the mixture is blue and yellow, with a larger admixture of the granules of silver, the whole surface being so brilliantly polished that each minute gem is distinctly seen. The pretty *P. speciosus* and *P. reticulatus* (Figs. 5 and 6) are also beautiful insects, from the excessive clearness of their markings and the high polish of their entire surface.

The native species, *Carabus intricatus* (Fig. 8), which has received its specific name from the intricacy of the tuberculations by which the surface of the elytra are variegated, was so rare a very few years ago that some considered it not truly indigenous; but it has since been captured in some numbers, in consequence of the discovery that moths were attracted by melted sugar brushed on the bark of trees at night, which happened to prove equally attractive to our night-roaming beetle, *Carabus intricatus*, and numbers were taken by the newly discovered bait. The "golden beetle," *Carabus auratus*, belongs to the same genus, and is perhaps the handsomest of the native *Carabi*. This species, like many of the *Carabi*, is carnivorous, and is called by the French *Le Jardinier*, as the enemy of cockchafers. It attacks the female when in the act of depositing her eggs, and so destroys at once a whole brood of those destructive insects. The *Carabidæ*, which are *carnivorous*, thus feed on other beetles which are *herbaceous* feeders, just as carnivorous quadrupeds prey upon those that are herbivorous.

The *Carabus Hispanus* (Fig. 9) is not indebted to a tropical sun for his superior brilliancy; for, on the contrary, his habitat is on the borders of eternal snow, in the Alpine regions of Central Europe. In the first place he is nearly twice the size of our native *Carabi*, but the size is his least attraction. It is in his brilliant metallic colours that his great beauty chiefly consists. The head and corslet are of the richest metallic purple, while the elytra, or wing-cases, are of the most dazzling olive gold, so solidly brilliant that chased and burnished metal itself could not surpass it. In the lights this golden glitter becomes a yellow, while in the shades it assumes a ruddy tone, becoming richly crimson in a narrow channel round the edges.

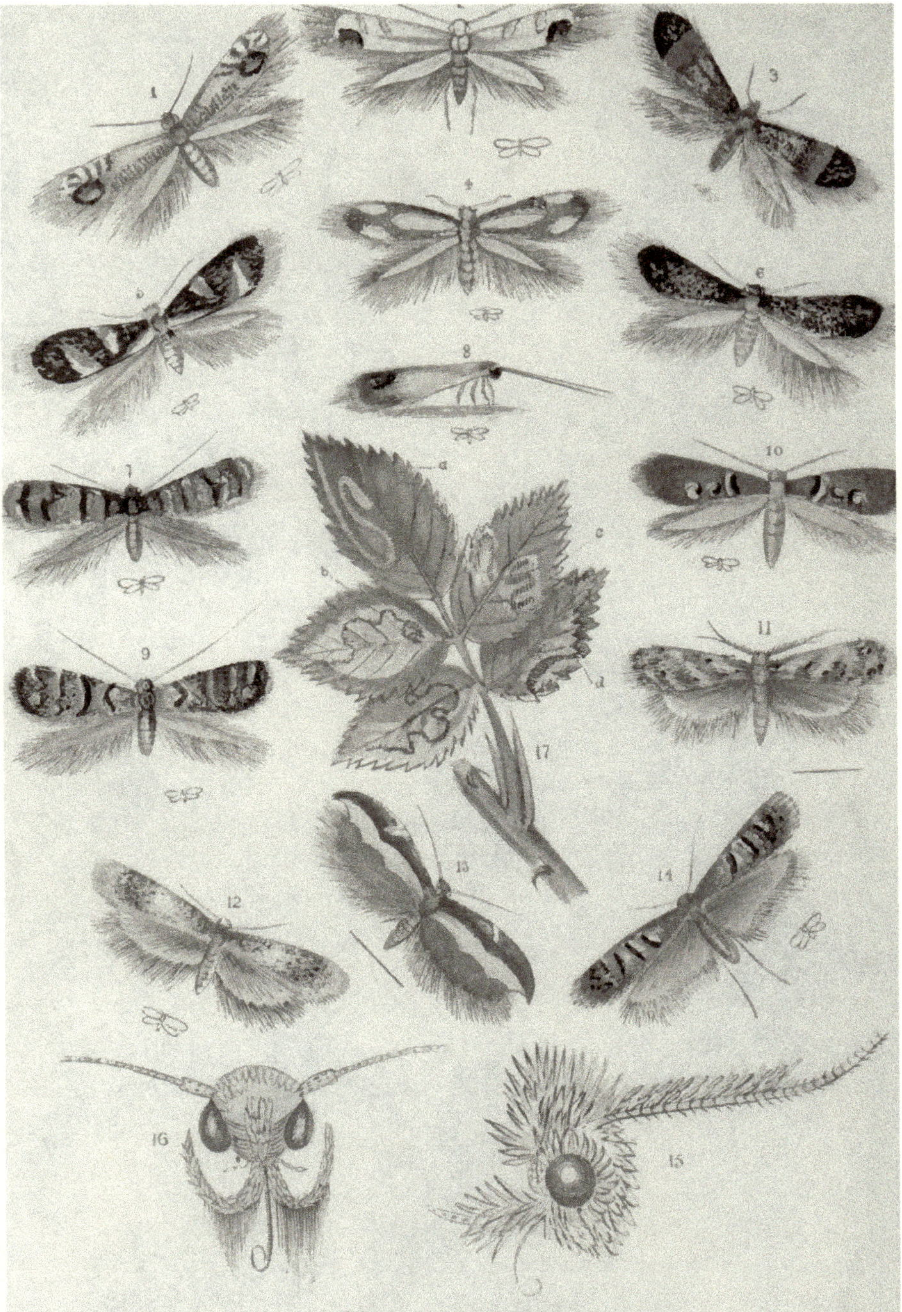

MICRO-LEPIDOPTERA,

(Leaf-Miners.)

1.—Cemiostoma scitella. *Hawthorn and Pear.*
2.—Cemiostoma laburnella. *Laburnum.*
3.—Nepticula aurella. *Blackberry.*
4.—Nepticula trimaculella. *Poplar.*
5.—Nepticula Subbimaculella. *Oak.*
6.—Nepticula Anomalella *Rose-leaf.*
7.—Lithocolletis stettinensis. *Alder.*
8.—Tischeria marginea. *Bramble.*
9.—Glyphipteryx equitella. *Stonecrop.*
10.—Elachista luticomella. *Dactylis glomerata.*
11.—Ochsenheimeria. *Dactylis glomerata.*
12.—Gelechia Malvella. *Hollyhock*
13.—Cerostoma Xylostella. *Honeysuckle.*
14.—Gelechia Hermanella. *Chenopodium.*
15.—Head of Ochsenheimeria.
16.—Coriscium. *Oak.*

All these figures are highly magnified. The natural size is given in the lines beneath each, or in a minute figure.

17.—Examples of different larva mines. *a*, mine of Nepticula aurella on the *Bramble*. *b*, mine of the Nepticula anomalella on the *Rose-leaves*. *c*, mine of Nepticula viscerella on the *Elm*. *d*, mine

THE MICRO-LEPIDOPTERA, OR LEAF-MINERS.

But few observers have devoted any attention to these interesting moths, although of such beautiful hues and metallic lustre, glorious as the Admiral and Peacock butterflies in the variety and richness of their colouring, whilst in their instincts they are as wonderful as any of their larger brethren. Messrs. Stainton, Zeller, and Douglas, who have applied themselves to the study of these minute Lepidoptera, have recorded their researches in magnificent volumes almost unattainable to ordinary lovers of entomology. In our plate we give representations of our commonest leaf-miners, highly magnified, the natural size being indicated by minute figures or by lines beneath; and in this chapter we shall describe them and their haunts and habits to assist the young student in his research.

"It was one of the wonders of my childhood," says Mrs. Lane Clarke, "what the hieroglyphics upon primrose, bramble, and rose leaves could possibly mean. I saw a white winding stream meandering along with a dark wavy line in the centre, beginning at a mere speck and swelling into a broad river, then suddenly ending. Holding a rose leaf to the light, one day, there was life within that winding way, a sheltered, naked little worm sustained in the narrow channel between the upper and lower cuticle of the leaf; food, safety, warmth, all provided within the limits of the rose-leaf mine. Picking open the upper skin and finding a small green caterpillar, curious to know its metamorphosis, and failing to preserve the larvæ in the gathered leaves, I bethought me of muslin bags, which I tied over the twigs of rose trees and brambles, laburnums and lilacs, which were the first mined and rolled leaves I had observed; and great was my joy when from these pages of nature's own book I first learnt the mysteries of the microscopic moths. Every folded leaf is in truth the habitation of the larva of a minute Lepidoptera, and beneath the leaf a blotch, a pucker, or a tiny tent, will, if watched, produce one of these beautiful objects. Scientifically they are divided into leaf-miners, leaf-rollers, tent-makers, and burrowers in the stems of the plant whereon they feed. Not *all* leaf-miners produce Lepidoptera, for several of the Diptera begin life in the same way. The primrose, whose leaves are often covered with irregular, fantastic markings, feeds the larvæ of a small, striped, greyish black fly with yellow legs (*Phytomyza primula*). The thistle is mined by a yellow and black fly (*Phytomyza sonchi*). The turnip and pea by the little yellow *Drasophila*. The plantain, ranunculus, stellaria, lychnis, chenopodium, and silene, are all mined by *Phytomyzides*. The iris, verbascum, euphorbia, by *Agromyzides*, very minute black or black and yellow flies, some of them with bright red eyes, but so small as to be really microscopic; not one line in expansion, yet sad devastators in the garden are they."

But the larva of a Diptera may always be distinguished from that of the Lepidoptera, at least under the microscope, by the absence of feet in the dipterous larva, and the presence, however minute or rudimentary, of these organs in the lepidopterous larva. Sometimes, it is true, the undeveloped condition of the true legs, and the absence in all leaf-miners of the coronet of hooks upon the pro-legs, or membranous feet on the hinder segments of the body, may cause a doubt, as it did in the mind of the great naturalist De Geer, when on finding the rose-leaf miner and examining the larvæ, he wrote:—"After examining their figure and the conformation of some of their parts, one would only take them to be *vers* or dipterous larvæ, because they have eighteen legs, all membranous and alike in form, exactly like the legs of *Fausses-chenilles*, or larvæ of saw-flies; that is to say, without the coronet of hooks which distinguishes the true caterpillars. I thought therefore at first that these were a new species of dipterous larvæ. Sometimes I was inclined to consider them the larvæ of saw-flies, but as they had no horny legs, it seemed to me that they could not belong to these insects. In fact, I persisted in the opinion that my leaf-miners were dipterous larvæ, till they assumed their last form—till they showed me that they changed into true moths." It was of the rose-leaf miner (*Nepticula anomella*, Fig. 6) that De Geer wrote thus, and it renders the species particularly interesting when we know that it was the first of the miners which attracted his particular attention, and subsequently led our own naturalists, Westwood and Stainton, to the study of the Micro-Lepidoptera. The little moth itself is frequently found on our windows in the early spring, the dark grey or bronzy wings tipped with violet, and silvery grey under-wings, deeply fringed with delicate cilia, or minute moving organs resembling hairs. All these microscopic moths are remarkable for the extraordinary size of their scales, and many of them for the rich metallic lustre, iridescent as the scales of a diamond beetle.

Cemiostoma scitella (Fig. 1) is a lovely microscopic moth, which those who live in or near London will find no difficulty in watching during its development and securing specimens of, for the larva is abundant in July and August, disfiguring the leaves of hawthorn, apple, and pear, with irregular flat brown blotches, and if we hold one of the leaves to the light, the little miner may be seen feeding busily. Also upon a still evening, or on the sheltered side of a hedge, we find in the month of June numbers of the small grey moths creeping slowly about the leaves depositing eggs. Their minute size renders the exceeding beauty of their wings indiscernible to the naked eye, and it is difficult to mount them without ruffling their delicate wings. This is just one of those surprises which an observant mind obtains, when in a mere dot of life such elaborate finish and perfection is discovered. A little creeping ashen-grey moth spreads a pair of upper wings clothed with feathery scales, that require the utmost power of human skill in microscopic lenses to investigate. On the membrane of this wing, which has a definite tracery of veins marking the species, there are rows of cup-like sockets into which each tiny scale is fitted securely for the insect's flight, but which will not bear the coarse touch of human fingers. These scales, invisible to the naked eye, are composed of three distinct laminæ, two external and coloured, the inner one a highly polished colourless membrane, which reflects the light and increases the brilliancy of each scale. The wing of this little *Cemiostoma*, shining with the silvery grey mass of microscopic feathers, has a large black spot with violet eye, and streaks of purest white, and deepest black, radiating off into the long silken fringe that is so remarkably beautiful in all these moths. The egg, strangely large for the size of the moth, is laid on the under side of a leaf, and the larva, as soon as hatched, bores through the cuticle and eats away a cavern in the parenchyma or cellular tissue, which daily spreads into a large blotch, brown at first but afterwards white, with markings of black in half circles, which is the excrement of the worm as it works from side to side. When full fed it comes out at the upper side of the leaf, and spins a pretty white cocoon, leaving a slit at one end, through which it rejects the cast-off skin when assuming the pupa state, and by which the little moth eventually comes forth.

Cemiostoma laburnella (Fig 2) is a delicate white moth, with violet pupil on its wings, and should be mounted on a blue disc, for then the dark radiating streaks in the cilia will be more distinctly seen.

There is another moth, *Cemiostoma spartifolia*, which mines the *twig*, not the leaf, of the common broom, and so like the *Laburnella* that only a practised eye can discern the slightest difference, although there is invariably one slight variation marking its individuality, for the wing of *C. laburnella* has three *parallel* lines passing from the second yellow dot through the cilia, while the wing of *C. spartifolia* has three *converging* strokes from the same dot. Two broods in the year spoil our laburnum leaves in appearance, but not in reality; for although the little insect feeds upon the pulp of the leaf, the veins or channels of the sap are not injured, and the tree itself does not suffer in vitality, at least to any great degree. The first brood come forth from the mine in July to spin cocoons, and fasten them to branches of the tree; but the second brood in October descend by little silken ropes, and hide themselves amongst dead leaves, spinning pure white cocoons, firm and warm, wherein to sleep securely through the long winter.

Nepticula aurella (Fig. 3) is the most minute of all the Micro-Lepidoptera, and the most easily observed, as it mines our rose leaves and brambles, but is by no means easy to catch, for it runs with wonderful rapidity. Though it may be found at rest on palings or trunks of trees, yet it is wary, flits off at an approach, and the delicate wings will be damaged by the sweep of a net; and it is, therefore, better to breed specimens by collecting the cocoons, or enclosing a bramble branch in a muslin bag. The cocoons are always found in groups of about twenty, though the larvæ are quite solitary in their spinning and feeding.

Nepticula trimaculella (Fig. 4) is a pretty spotted moth, which may be found resting on the trunks of oak trees in all parts of England, about May and June. The larva, which is green and shining, with a reddish head, and red dorsal vessel, pulsating visibly under the microscope, mines oak leaves in a blotch about an inch long, close to the mid-rib, from which it issues to spin a pale, yellow, mussel-shaped cocoon. The *Nepticulæ* always mine the *upper* side of leaves, except this species, which is sometimes found on the *under* side.

Nepticula sub-bimaculella (Fig. 5) is another little oak-miner, but producing only one brood, is only in the larva state in October, making a triangular blotch in an angle between the mid-rib and one of the veins of the leaf. The egg having been laid on the *upper* side of the leaf close to the mid-rib, the larva keeps very close to the rib, leaving a thick, black, central line of excrement; after which it turns about and eats out a blotch, in which, as it grows, the excrement is deposited in grains; from which observations it appears that the excrement is always fluid in the early stage of larva life, and becomes solid as the digestive organs develop.

Nepticula anomalella (Fig. 6) is the little moth that attracted the notice of De Geer. Specimens can be readily found upon rose trees in July and October, mining in serpentine galleries the *under* side of the leaf, but coming out at the upper side, and spinning a cocoon at the footstalk of a leaf, or under a projecting thorn. There is another leaf-miner on the rose, *N. Anguli-fasciella*, much prettier, having dark wings, and a curved silver band across; and in the larva state they may be distinguished by the *Anomalella* being amber-coloured, and the other of a pale green. Three or four of these little miners are often found on the same leaf, in which case they cross each other's path, and make the tracing of a single mine rather difficult.

Lithocolletis stetinensis (*Argyromiges*) (Fig. 7) is a beautiful moth, one of a family containing seventy species, so delicately small, and yet so brilliant, that naturalists have called them the humming-birds of the Lepidoptera. The larvæ are extremely abundant on the elm, maple, honeysuckle, scabious, oak, and nut trees. Some species mine the upper and some the lower cuticle of a leaf. It is found that the larva of a *Lithocolletis never quits its mine*, but changes therein to a pupa; and the empty pupa-skin may be found protruding from a slit in the cuticle after the escape of the perfect insect. The *Nepticulæ* always emerge from the mine, and fix themselves to a stalk or a dead leaf for transformation. There is but one exception, and that is with *Nepticula septembrella*, which mines the leaves of *Hypericum pulchrum* (small upright St. John's wort) in autumn, making extremely slender mines around and across the small leaves; when full fed, they pucker the leaf a little, and form a cocoon inside the mine. Again, the larva of a *Lithocolletis* more or less contorts the leaf, which *Nepticula* does not, and carpets the loosened cuticle with silk, pulling it so tight that not only does the skin pucker, but the opposite side of the leaf is drawn into a curve.

Tischeria marginea (Fig. 8), a pretty moth, may be seen in May and August flitting over the brambles, or, as in the plate, sitting with folded wings, closely pressed to the substance upon which it rests, with its head slightly raised, and long antennæ thrown forward. The bright yellow dot of life is absorbed in the work of depositing its eggs on the under side of the blackberry leaves, which will soon have the tracery of a little mine, resembling a *cornucopia*, and puckered at the widest part because the *Tischeria* does not quit that shelter, but changes to a pupa in its mine. Side by side we may observe the more wavy and intricate hieroglyphic of the *Nepticula*, and compare the larva. The moth is four lines long.

Glyphipteryx equitella is not a leaf-miner, but a *burrower*, and with a truly microscopic beauty, for the exquisite markings of its wings are never well seen except with a pocket lens or a three-inch object-glass. The dark bronzy-grey ground is streaked with pure white, edged with silver; two violet-silvery spots in the middle, and another at the tip, near which a hook of jet-black scales project through the cilia. This moth flies over the stonecrop in June, where it deposits the eggs, from whence a little miner comes forth to plunge into the stem, and work away in a channel through which it revels in the ascending sap.

Elachista luticomella (Fig. 10), though but little known till recently, may be seen in swarms on summer evenings hovering over their favourite *Dactylis glomerata*, or Cocksfoot-grass, which feeds the young larvæ. Stainton names forty species of the grass-miners, which, when full grown, quit the mine, and attach themselves to the stem of a neighbouring plant. They fix their bodies by a silken belt like the cabbage caterpillar, and change to an angulated pupa.

Ochsenheimeria (Fig. 11) is properly not a microscopic moth, for it is from five to six lines in expansion, and not particularly beautiful; but the head (Fig. 15) is most curious, and deserves observation. Its feathered antennæ and bird-like eyes are unlike all other moths. It can be caught only in the hottest part of the day, from 12 A.M. to 2 P.M., when it hops about the grass, depositing eggs on the *Dactylis glomerata*. It is marvellously quick in hiding away, and if not swept into the net whilst on the wing, will not be easily secured.

The *Gelechidæ* have varied habits, for the larvæ of many of them feed between the united leaves of sallows, honeysuckle, firs, oaks, and apple trees. *G. malvella* (Fig. 12) devours the seeds of the hollyhock; but *G. hermanella* (Fig. 14) is a true leaf-miner. The larvæ make dirty green blotches on the leaves of the *Chenopodium*, or Fat-hen, and *Atriplex*, and the moth, flitting over these plants in July and October, is of a bright orange red, flaked with silvery streaks, and set off by jet-black scales. These moths are scarcely microscopic, being from six to nine lines in expansion.

Cerastoma xylostella (Fig. 13) measures ten lines across the outstretched wings, yet it belongs to the Micro-Lepidoptera, and its larva, bright green, with scarlet stripe along its back, will in July be feeding on the honeysuckle.

The beautiful plumed head of the *Ochsenheimeria* (Fig. 15), and the head of *Coriscium* (Fig. 16), an oak-leaf miner, plentiful in April, June, August, and September, with drooping and tufted palpi, show us the minute yet decided variations which mark the species.

Examples of different larva mines are represented in Fig. 17. "Pondering on the hieroglyphics these little miners trace," says Mrs. Lane Clarke, "words of infinite wisdom to the eye that can read and the heart that can understand; seeing how in darkness yet perfect security the naked worm feeds, grows, and develops a new and wondrous beauty of which it is wholly unconscious, and of which for thousands of years man was profoundly ignorant; we pause reverently before the tracery on a rose leaf, the blotch on the laburnum, and we look beyond the present mystery of our own life, oftentimes a dark and a winding way, with a hope strengthened in looking at the glorious wings of the hitherto scarcely appreciated Microscopic Moth."

1
2
3
4
5
6
7
8 b
6-a
10

THE COLEOPHORA, OR TENT-MAKERS.

The Coleophora are a genus of the Micro-Lepidoptera. The moths are not nearly so beautiful as the *Nepticulæ* and *Lithocolletis* described in the preceding chapter. Their wings are lanceolated, or shaped like a lance, of one colour, or striped with silken grey under-wings, and they sit with bodies closely pressed to the substance on which they rest, with their antennæ thrown forward, much like the *Tischeriæ*. But the larvæ of this genus manifest an instinct and design which open for us a delightful field of observation. They feed upon the parenchyma or cellular tissue of leaves, and mine irregular blotches as they feed; but with the cuticle, or leaf itself, or husk of seed, they fashion tents, under which they walk about, and within which they retire when the time of pupa rest has come, and the resurrection into perfect life is at hand.

The Coleophora may be collected from June to October. When you find a blotched or mined leaf with a round hole, as truly outlined as if drilled with a centre-bit, you may be sure that a Coleophora has been feeding there, and this little hole was the entrance into its pasture-ground, covered closely by its tent, whilst the owner penetrated into the soft, juicy parenchyma, and stretched away, as far as its body would reach, on all sides, careful only to keep its anal hooks at the tent-door to secure a retreat on the least alarm.

"These tiny caterpillars," says Mrs. Lane Clarke, "scarcely noticed by the unassisted eye, are wonderful in their instinct, as the *Lithocolletis* are marvellous in their beauty. Here is a mere speck, a little brown naked worm, busy on the leaf before me; nothing can be more insignificant in appearance, or more unworthy of minute attention; hardly does the careless eye perceive it, and yet how the detail of its structure reveals the mind of its Great Creator; the same wisdom planning, and the same goodness adapting, each organ for the tiny workman that has given to man his more perfect body. Look closely at the larva itself before we describe its proceedings. Externally we observe a small black head, with six simple eyes in a circle on each side, a pair of sharp-toothed jaws, four little palps or feelers, and a spinnaret immediately under the jaws; six true legs and ten membranous appendages, thirteen joints or segments, and on each segment a spiracle dilating and contracting as the larva breathes and moves. At the anal segment there is a protuberance, armed with hooks, which it uses as a claw to attach itself to the leaf whilst making its case, and afterwards as a grappling-iron to retain possession of its tenement."

The preparation of the *Cossus ligniperda*, or Goat-Moth, by Mr. Robertson, in the Oxford Museum, in illustration of Lyonnet's researches, proves the existence of 4,061 muscles in that caterpillar, 228 being attached to the head, 1,647 to the body, and 2,186 to the intestines. This is one of the largest of the British Moths, measuring from tip to tip of the wings when expanded from 3 inches to 3¾. The larva when full grown is about 3 inches in length; and when we consider that "we have no reason whatever for denying the same number of muscular bands to the smallest larva, and that the Coleophora in particular has need of every kind of muscle in the fashioning and bearing about its tent, a feeling of positive awe steals over the mind. Every kind of muscle! Yes—levators, depressors, flexors, extensors, abductors, adductors, supinators, and pronators. We need but watch the persistent action of those busy jaws to be very sure that its abductors and adductors are in perfection; whilst to twist about its spinnaret and weave the tapestry of its chamber, supinators and pronators must be in full play, as well as the ceaseless constrictor muscles, opening and closing the spiracles, and giving such varied movements to the segments of the abdomen. Would the dorsal vessel pulsate without that arrangement of muscular fibre, by which the systole and diastole is maintained? and would the peristaltic motion, so necessary to digestion, go on without that exquisite network of innumerable muscular threads, which twine along, and across, and around every internal organ? No; all this mystery of life goes on planned, directed, and sustained beneath the tegument of this microscopic worm.

"Now what is the little larva about? I have placed it under the microscope; it has at length entered the leaf, and eaten more than the length and breadth of its body. I turned it out of its case at 2 P.M. It wandered restlessly until 4 P.M., then fixed and opened its circular door, slowly going forward, until on my return at 10 P.M. it had advanced into perfect shelter. The next morning a large blotch was eaten, but I was in time to sit beside the elm-branch and watch the making of the tent. It had fixed near the edge of the leaf, and was carefully eating out the parenchyma of each serrature, leaving the edges untouched, as it thereby saved a seam in the tent, yet emptying each tooth to make it light and less brittle. When all was clear, the larva measured a gentle curve a little larger than its body, and began to draw the cuticle together on the opposite side to the serratures—tacking it loosely at first, and biting the membrane between the fibres, sewing it more neatly then, and careful not to cut the supporting braces formed by the nerves of the leaf. Then it rubbed the interior of the case with its head, as if to smooth it, and presently began to darken it with a web of fine silk, rendering further operations invisible, only I perceived that one end was left open for the ejection of its excrement, and that the fibres were cut mysteriously away, when the tent by powerful muscular action was raised from the leaf, and the Coleophora marched off to refresh itself in a new excavation. Yet that was another point on which to rest and ponder. What was it eating, and how much did it eat? What store of delicate and varied food lies in the cells of any leaf; sugar and starch and chloraphyll, oils and gums and raphides; ay, and in some plants, like the common nettle, beautiful crystals suspended from the cell-wall, or floating about; sweetmeats and candies for the little gourmand—no wonder it eats so much; in twelve hours it ate the weight of its own body; as if a man should in the same time demolish thirty four-pound loaves of bread."

This formation of a tent at the edge of a leaf is not a mere routine of instinct, for Réaumur tested the resources of one of the same *Limosipennella* (Fig. 8) by turning one out to make a new case, and when the excavation was completed, cutting off the teeth of the leaf. The two membranes flew apart, and the little larva seemed to be surprised and troubled; after a little hesitation apparently it saw the remedy, turned itself about, and threw a few threads from side to side, pulled them close and joined the rent. Then, as if considering that a like misfortune might happen again, before proceeding in the work of mining necessary for a full-sized case, it darkened the interior of the mine with a regular silken tube, which it left to continue and mine in a curve directly down the leaf and across the fibres. Now and then it returned to the tube, and lengthened and strengthened that; yet with strange forethought the case was not woven throughout; one side was merely tacked together and spaces left by which the larva could put out its head and cut the leaf between the fibres which now supported the case, yet somehow perceiving that from the cutting away of the edge the natural curve was destroyed, the larva actually changed the aperture from one end to the opposite, in order to obtain the proper and convenient shape. At last, after two days' hard work, the tent was finished, and the thoughtful, patient little architect went on its way towards the development and perfection of its being.

The *Coleophora Vitella*, whose tent is given in Fig. 2, may be found as early as April, having begun its case from the leaf of *Vaccinium vitis idæa* (cranberry) in the autumn, and up to the end of the month the case is being continually enlarged with pieces of the mined leaf, giving it a wrinkled appearance, and making it paler near the mouth as fresh bits are added, and the case becomes pistol-shaped. The moth comes out at the end of June, and is abundant near Manchester.

Coleophora laricella (Fig. 4*a*) is a very small pretty little tent-maker, and feeds on the tenderest shoots of the larch in early spring time. It is hatched in the autumn, and mining a slender leaf cuts it off and hoists it as a tent for its shelter and defence, remaining asleep in it all the winter, and with the first warmth of April, and with the cuckoo's note, awakening to feed on the under side of the fresh green leaves. The mine is very transparent, and the proceedings of the caterpillar easily observed. The moth is all of one colour, a light brown with silky grey under-wings; and is plentiful at Guildford, Manchester, York, and in Scotland.

The *Coleophora juncicolella* (Fig. 5) may be found on the heights of Dover, making its tent on the tufts of heath, with seven or nine little leaves, nor more nor less. Some are withered and reddish-brown or yellow, and the lower ones are green, so making a parti-coloured tent. The moth is small and grey-winged.

Coleophora Muripennella (Fig. 6*a*) may be found in the seed-vessels of the luzula, in June, near London, Lewes, Worthing, York, Scarborough, and in Scotland, and the delicately striped brown moth is abundant from April to June.

Coleophora Curricepennella (Fig. 7), a pretty striped moth, is more abundant abroad than in England, yet it is found near London and Wimbledon in May and June, producing a larva which weaves a case entirely of silk, quite black, and with four projections, diminishing towards the mouth, and one row forming a right-angle with another row. It eats the leaf so delicately that the parenchyma is removed, and the perfect network of fine veins left unbroken.

Coleophora lineola (Fig. 9) will repay the trouble of hunting for it on the underside of *Ballota nigra* (black horehound), or *Lamium purpurea* (purple dead nettle), and if you see some whity-brown, glassy-looking blotches in September, on these leaves, look under the leaf, and you will most likely find quite a little company of them on a single leaf.

The *Coleophora discordella* (Fig. 10) is found on grassy banks where the *Lotus corniculatus* grows, busily employed in adding piece after piece to his tent, which curves over like a reversed cornucopia. This larva feeds in August, and a silvery-striped pretty moth comes forth in June, for, like most of these case-bearers, it has a long larva-life of nearly nine months, hybernating in the cold winter, and recommencing active life in the spring.

The entomological student may look for various species of tent-makers on the following plants:—

On the Rushes	*C. cæspititiella.*
On Silene inflata . . .	*C. inflata.*
On Furze buds	*C. albicosta.*
On Knapweed	*C. conspicuella.*
On Stellaria Holastea .	*C. solitariella.*
On the Sallow	*C. viminetella.*
On Wormwood	*C. ditella.*
On Cistus	*C. ochrea.*

References to Plate.

Fig. 1. *Coleophora chalcogrammella.* 1*a*. Larva-tent feeding on *Cerastium arvense.* 2. Tent of *Coleophora Vitella.* 3. Larva of Coleophora. 4. Shoots of larch with larva of *C. laricella.* 4*a*. The tent of *C. laricella* magnified. 5. Tent of *C. juncicolella* on heath. 5*a*. The same magnified. 6. Tent of *Coleophora Muripennella.* 6*a*. The same magnified. 7. *Coleophora Curricepennella.* 7*a*. The tent of the same magnified. 8. Elm leaf with tents of *Coleophora Limosipennella.* 8*a*. A tent just cut from the leaf. 8*b*. The larva walking off with its tent. 9. The tent of *Coleophora lineola.* 10. The tent of *Coleophora discordella.*

THE MAY FLY.—GREEN AND GREY DRAKE.

(*Ephemera vulgata.*)

THE EPHEMERA, OR MAY-FLY.

This beautiful insect, the delight of the trout fisher, is so called from the Greek ἐφήμερα, living for a day. The family of *Ephemiridæ* consist of several genera, the generic characters of which are taken from the number of wings, and the setæ, or hair-like appendages to the abdomen. These setæ are of great use to the little insect in steering its way through the air whilst performing that beautifully undulating flight which all must have observed. The *Ephemeræ* have long, soft, tapering bodies, terminating in three long setæ, and four wings placed nearly or quite perpendicularly. Their antennæ are very small and three-pointed. The setæ are longer in the male, which is also readily distinguished from the female by longer fore-feet; the colour of the male is much darker than that of the female, being bronze or chocolate; and the male is also much smaller. The ovaries consist of two almond-shaped organs, which occupy nearly the whole of the abdominal cavity. The ova are unattached, and readily separate themselves in water. It is the possession of these ovaries that makes the insects such fat delicacies for the hungry fish which feed on them. The eggs, having been deposited in the water, sink to the bottom, and change into a small larva, in which state it is said to live for two or three years, under water or in wet places, and then to change to the *nympha*. Both in its larval and nymphal condition the creature eats, and the intestinal canal is found to contain numerous algæ spores, small crustacea, rotifera, &c.

The larvæ and nymphæ are often found in holes in the river banks, and frequently also in the sand or mud at the bottom of the water. The only difference between the larva and nympha is that the latter has sheaths for the wings, which are rolled or crumpled up inside them. The banks of rivers may often be seen to be completely riddled by these larvæ, which tunnel for themselves tubular galleries in the mud to the depth of four or five inches. The larvæ of some other members of the Ephemeridæ, instead of living under the sand, or in tubular galleries, swim from place to place, as in the genus *Cloë*, while others crawl on the ground and on aquatic plants. In throwing off their swaddling-clothes the Ephemeræ emerge through a split in the back. They often draw out the anterior part of the body first, and sometimes the tail part, or abdomen, appears first. Sometimes, instead of leaving their swaddling-clothes in the water, they deposit them on a blade of grass, or some water-weed. Being heavy fliers in their sub-imago state—for their wings are scarcely dry, and their muscles unequal as yet to any great exertion—they are constantly dropping for a second or two on the water, and are then sucked down the throat of some fish.

The Rev. W. Houghton thus describes the further metamorphosis:—"Let us now follow the green-drake to the spot where he has rested. Here he will remain for the space of two or three hours, perhaps, and then will be introduced to the world of life as an adult and perfect insect. Look at this blade of grass. What is the shadowy form that clings to it? It is a delicate membrane, thin and light as possible, which the slightest breath will blow away. Notice the split across the back, through which the former tenant left his abode. It is the cast-off skin of the green-drake, now metamorphosed into a creature more active than Harlequin or Columbine—the male into a dark-brown insect, with clear and gauze-like wings, the female into a beautiful creature, with body marbled white and brown. How different now is the mode of flight! But, alas, 'out of the frying-pan into the fire.' The flies are partly safe from Scylla, but they fall into Charybdis; for birds of various kinds, swallows, swifts, tom-tits, larks, chaffinches, and a host of other feathered enemies, are on the watch, seeking the dainty morsels to feed themselves or their hungry young. See now how curious is the dance they practise. Up and down, up and down! with head erect, and bodies prettily curving upwards, dancing in the sun, which now shines out from beneath the clouds—merrily, merrily! Truly an *Ephemera's* life has many 'ups and downs,' and the insects doubtless enjoy them immensely. But we must here notice that it is the males that execute this particular style of dance, rising up sometimes ten or twelve feet, then dropping down suddenly the same distance. At least, I am inclined to think this dancing is confined to the gentlemen; for I have never yet detected a lady, in her white and marble dress, amongst the company. The flight of her ladyship differs considerably now from what it was before she cast her last garments away. No longer a clumsy, helpless mode of flying, sustained with much difficulty; but a swift, strong flight, not unlike that of the dragon-fly, is that of the perfect Ephemeral imago. Now high in the air, now sailing along close to the surface of the water, ever and anon dipping gently into it, she is evidently busy discharging some important duty. She is laying her eggs, by little packets at a time, first in one place and then in another. The small oval eggs sink quickly down to the bottom, and attach themselves to submerged weeds and stones. This is the sole object of her life, now that she has become a mother; not a particle of food has she tasted since she left her nymphal state, not a particle of food will she taste so long as her short life lasts. If you examine the digestive apparatus of any of these insects, whether male or female, when in the imago or sub-imago state, you will never find the slightest traces of food in the stomach; this organ, as well as the whole intestinal canal, is almost always full of air-bubbles; catch one of those dancing males with their long extended fore-feet, that you may mistake for antennæ, and press him quickly in the middle, crack he goes, for the little air-bubbles have burst by the pressure. No wonder that *Ephemera's* stomach is empty, for he has no mouth, at least none that could be of any use to him; so rudimentary is that organ now. The intestinal canal, there can be no doubt, serves the purpose of buoying up the little animal, and saves the expenditure of muscular action; for as no food is taken to supply the waste, the muscles will not be capable of long-sustained action."

When they attain their final stage of metamorphosis and perfect form, they are among the most fleeting of living creatures, existing often for only a few hours, and propagating their species before they die. In this state they sometimes appear suddenly in myriads, during fine summer evenings, by the water-side, where they may be seen flitting about and balancing themselves in the air, in the manner of gadflies. But the term *Ephemera*, so applicable to this creature of a day, must not be understood in too restricted a sense. It is quite true that numbers are devoured by fishes or birds before their final change is effected, and that the survivors have but a very brief existence. After the laying of the eggs, which, however, may last more than a single day, the female perishes, or dies a natural death. The only business of her life being accomplished, she has now only to die. If, however, a specimen be caught, and kept in confinement, and the laying be thus checked, an Ephemera may live several days. Whether the males are as short-lived as the females, we cannot say, but it is not improbable that they may survive somewhat longer, though, from the fact of their taking no food, it is probable that the life of all the *Ephemeræ* is very short.

The figure on the left-hand blade of grass in the coloured plate represents the female green-drake, which changes into the grey-drake, seen resting on the right-hand blade, leaving her cast-off pellicle upon the grass stem. The flying insect is the perfect male.

That the grey-drake is only the female green-drake metamorphosed, or rather after the last pellicle is cast, may be sometimes readily proved by dissection. The marble and white skin of the female grey-drake may be seen by carefully slitting open or peeling off the first integument of the green-drake.

The expressions green and grey-*drakes*, as applied to the May-flies by anglers, owe their origin to the fact that the wings of the artificial fly are made from a mallard's feather, dyed olive for the green-drake, or immature condition of the insect; and from the same feather, slightly stained with purple, for the grey-drake, or perfect form of the female. The term May-fly is very indefinite, standing for all sorts of different insects in different counties.

In this country, the May-flies appear about the end of May and the beginning of June, and continue for about three weeks. The green-drake issues from his nymphal state almost at any hour in the day, but especially when the sun is shining. In Sweden, the birth of these insects is confined nearly to the evening, about sunset; but it is quite an error to assert that our British *Ephemera vulgata* emerges from the water only in the evening. Some species of Ephemeridæ appear in the most astonishing swarms, in some parts of Europe. Scopoli tells us, that so great an abundance of *E. vulgata* sometimes occurs near the Lake Laz, in the month of June, that the inhabitants of the district are quite disappointed if they do not collect twenty cartloads of insects for manure! "Between the 10th and 15th of August is the time when those of the Seine and the Marne, which Réaumur described, are expected by the fishermen, who call them *manna;* and when their season is come, they say, 'The manna begins to appear; the manna fell abundantly such a night.'" These immense swarms of *Ephemeridæ* have been noticed in Holland, Switzerland, and France, and have been compared to falling flakes of snow. "The myriads of *Ephemeræ* which filled the air," says Réaumur, "over the current of the river, and over the bank on which I stood, are neither to be expressed nor conceived. When the snow falls with the largest flakes, and with the least interval between them, the air is not so full of them as that which surrounded the *Ephemeræ*." The occurrence of such countless swarms of *Ephemeridæ* is unknown in the British Isles.

MIMETIC ANALOGY,

ILLUSTRATED BY SOUTH AMERICAN BUTTERFLIES.

MIMETIC ANALOGY is a term used to express the extraordinary imitation by one animal of some other animal, which is most frequently of some other group. Sometimes the object imitated is inanimate, as a stone, a bud, a leaf, or a broken twig, instances of which are so common that they have been noticed by the most ordinary observers. "The greater number of animals," says Mr. Tegetmeier, "assume more or less closely the colour and appearance of the objects with which they are generally surrounded. Thus reptiles, such as frogs, snakes, &c., living on the ground, resemble the colour of objects on the earth's surface; whereas the tree-frogs are usually of a bright green colour, in accordance with the leaves amongst which they spend their lives. Even in birds of bright showy plumage, in which this assimilation of colours would hardly ever be suspected, it frequently prevails. Thus in the beautiful little Australian warbling parrakeets, known generally in this country by the aboriginal name of Betcherrygar, the resemblance of the colour to that of the leaves of the Eucalypti, or gum-tree, on which they repose during the mid-day heat, is so close, as Mr. Gould informs us, that though dozens may be perched on a branch, they are hardly to be observed when at rest. Among our own insects the imitation of inanimate objects is not unfrequent: the common buff-tip moth is a familiar example, as when at rest it closely resembles a piece of broken lichen-covered twig, the end of which is simulated by the tips of its closed wings. The use of the terms mimetic analogy and mimicry, as descriptive of these undeniable phenomena, has been strongly objected to

SOUTH AMERICAN BUTTERFLIES.

Illustrating Mimetic Analogy.

1. Leptalis Nehemia.	3. Leptalis Orise.
2. Leptalis Theonoë,	3a. Methona Psidii.
var. Leuconoë.	4. Leptalis Theonoë.
2a. Ithomia Herdina.	4a. Ithomia Flora.

by certain writers, who imagine that the words imply that the animals have power to change or alter their own condition. No supposition can be possibly more absurd. The change is not effected by the will of the individual animal, but occurs in the species; variations are involuntary, and at present even their very cause is unknown; all that is known is that they do occur both in wild and domestic animals, and that they are capable of hereditary transmission."

This imitation of natural objects is not confined to a few species; but has been observed in entire groups, and even in the whole insect fauna of a country at particular seasons. The Rev. Joseph Greene, writing on our autumnal and winter moths in the *Zoologist* for 1856, says: "I am not aware whether any entomologist has ever been struck by the singular adaptation and similarity of colouring in the autumnal and winter Lepidoptera to the prevailing tints of nature during these seasons. Counting from the middle of September, when the leaves begin to turn, to the end of February, we find among the Bombyces, Noctuæ, and Geometræ, about fifty-eight species on the wing. Now in the autumn the hue of nature is golden—she passes through all the intermediate stages from pale yellow to a deep rich brown; while in winter she assumes a grey or silvery garb. Taking those fifty-eight species, we find in their prevailing colours a striking and remarkable similarity to those which nature assumes at the time of their appearance in a winged state. Three species are doubtful, seven militate against my theory, the remainder are decidedly in my favour." He then proceeds to enumerate the autumnal species, which are yellow or rich brown, and the winter species, which are grey or silvery, and concludes:—"It certainly strikes me as a very interesting fact, showing the hand of an Almighty and Allwise Being to be visible in this as in all the other works of the Creation."

These imitations are not confined to the invertebrate animals or the lower forms of life, for there are examples of mimetic analogy among the warm-blooded vertebrata. Thus the grey-banded cuckoos so closely resemble hawks, both in appearance and flight, that they are constantly mistaken for them in all parts of the world, not only by the natives, but by the smaller birds of the several countries.

As it may be thought that these imitations are rather general and accidental, than particular and designed, we will quote a close and very remarkable example of imitation, described by Mr. Wallace, in the *Transactions* of the Zoological Society, who, when speaking of the birds newly discovered by him in the Mollucca Islands, observes, "that two species of the Oriolidæ, natives of Bouru and Ceram, departed altogether from the natural appearance of the group, and mimicked two species of Honeysuckers so closely as to deceive ordinary observers." Speaking of the birds inhabiting Bouru, he writes: "The oriole has departed from the usual gay colouring of its allies, and is actually the dullest coloured of its family, while the honeysucker that it imitates very much resembles in its colouration other species of the group to which it belongs. The imitation is carried to the minutest particulars; the black orbits of the honeysucker are copied by a patch of dusky feathers around the eyes of the oriole, and even the very peculiar ruff of recurved feathers on the nape of the former, has its general effect imitated by a collar of pale colour in the latter. The under and upper surfaces of the two birds are as near as possible of the same tint respectively, and, stranger still, the oriole has closely copied the mode of flight and voice of its model, so that in a state of nature the two birds are practically undistinguishable. This curious instance does not stand alone, for in the adjacent island of Ceram, two allied but very distinct species resemble each other with equal accuracy."

With regard to the object of this imitation, Mr. Wallace observes: "In the case of insects it seems probable that it is the odour or the taste of the imitated species which is unpalatable to insect-eating birds; or, in other cases, like the clear-winged moths, which mimic Hymenoptera, the species mimicked are armed with a sting. In birds, it is evident that the bravest, strongest, and best-armed groups should be the subjects of mimicry, and the weakest and most defenceless those which should obtain some advantage by imitating them.

"Returning to the oriole and the honeysucker, we have to observe that the former is a smaller, weaker, less active, less noisy, and less pugnacious bird. The feet have a less powerful grasp, and the bill is less acute. The latter has a great variety of loud and piercing notes, which bring its companions to the rescue in time of danger. And I have observed them drive away crows, and even hawks, which had ventured to perch on a tree where two or three of them were feeding. The honeysucker knows how to take care of himself, and make himself both respected and feared. It would, therefore, evidently be to the advantage of the more defenceless oriole to be mistaken for him.

"In this instance, as in most others, the imitation is far closer in the living bird than in the dead specimens. This is a far more satisfactory case of mimicry than any of those which I have before alluded to as occurring among birds. We have here two species, each confined to single islands, and each accurately imitated by a bird of a distinct family, with which it has no direct affinities. I therefore cannot doubt that this is a true case of mimicking exactly analogous to that so common among insects."

The most remarkable cases of mimetic analogy which have come to our knowledge are those of certain butterflies found in the valley of the Amazon. Mr. H. W. Bates investigated these cases most carefully, and recorded the results in the *Transactions* of the Linnæan Society, vol. xxiii., from which we give a summary of his observations.

Among the numerous butterflies of this region are various genera and species belonging to the family of Heliconidæ. They thrive and flourish although of feeble structure and slow in flight, and apparently without any means of defence in districts abounding with insect-eating birds, and are so numerous that the pathways of the forests are quite gay with the myriads that fly about clothed in bright orange, yellow, red, blue, and black. Some of the species are in the habit of assembling in small parties like our gnats, or by twos and threes, to sport together, and perform a kind of mazy dance. The sport generally begins with a single pair, which advance, retire, glide right and left in face of each other, wheel round to a considerable distance, again approach, and so on; then a third joins in, then a fourth, and others until a large party is assembled. They never touch; but when too many are congregated a general flutter ensues, and they all fly off to fall in again by pairs soon afterwards.

Wherever large numbers of these Heliconidæ are found, they are always accompanied by species which mimic them in size, form, colour, and marking, so closely that it is often impossible to distinguish one species from the other when they are on the wing, as the imitators fly in the same part of the forest, and usually accompany the species they imitate. To so wonderful a degree does this imitation extend, that in cases where there is a local variety of a species of this family, the butterfly imitating that particular species changes so as to follow the varieties of its model.

It may be asked, if two butterflies, of totally distinct groups, and different structures, so closely resemble one another, how can it be known which is the imitator and which the imitated? But the apparently puzzling question is easily answered. The imitated preserve the form and likeness peculiar to the family to which they belong; but the imitators are of a different aspect to their nearest allies. Thus when a clear-winged moth is found, bearing a close resemblance to any species of bee, it may be reasonably inferred that the moth, having departed from the usual aspect of its group, has imitated the bee, which remains like its congeners or fellows, and not that the bee has imitated the moth which differs from its species. For example, we are justified in assuming that the different species of Leptalis, shown in our plate (Figs. 2, 3, and 4), are the imitators, because they have departed from the proper normal form of the genus Leptalis which is shown in Fig. 1, representing *L. Nehemia;* and that the Heliconidæ there shown belonging to the genera Ithomia and Methona are the imitated, because they resemble their nearest allies. Hence we regard *Leptalis Theonoë,* var. Leuconoë (Fig. 2), as imitating *Ithomia Ilerdina* (Fig. 2*a*); *Leptalis Orise* (Fig. 3) as imitating *Methona Psidii*

(Fig. 3*a*); and *Leptalis Theonoë* (Fig. 4) as imitating *Ithomia Flora* (Fig. 4*a*). These resemblances are sufficiently striking even as shown in our plate, and still more so when observed in preserved specimens in the cabinet; but it is only when the insects are viewed in their natural state that the palpable intentional imitation is fully seen; for those features are most developed by nature which produce the most effective deception when the insects are seen alive.

The object to be gained by this imitation is evident in the majority of cases—protection against natural enemies either by concealment or disguise. Those animals that resemble the objects with which they are surrounded, are protected from the observation of others that prey upon them. The ground feeding birds, such as the partridge and snipe, the hare amidst dried leaves, the ptarmigan in the snow, the ermine in its winter dress, are all well-known instances of the advantage of the assimilation of colour to that of surrounding objects. In the case of the South American butterflies, the imitation is obviously for the purpose of disguise rather than that of concealment. The Heliconidæ are a numerous and flourishing group; and, although slow in flight, are never persecuted by birds or dragon-flies, to which it might be supposed they would be an easy prey; nor, when at rest on the leaves, are they molested by lizards or predaceous flies which constantly devour butterflies of other families. The Heliconidæ seem to owe their safety to their offensive odour, which renders them unpalatable to the enemies of insects; and even when set out to dry in the cabinet, they are less liable than other specimens to the attacks of vermin. Now it is obvious that the more closely an inodorous butterfly of another species resembles one of the offensive and unpalatable Heliconidæ, the less likely will it be to be preyed upon by its natural enemies, which is evidently the cause of the imitations of the genera Ithomia and Methona by the persecuted insects of the genus Leptalis.

Naturalists differ in opinion as to the origin of these resemblances. "Some naturalists," says Mr. Tegetmeier, "maintain that the resemblances existed from the Creation;

but the difficulties in this view of the case are numerous. One of the strongest arises from the fact, that in those cases where a local variation of the imitated animal exists, the imitator also varies to keep up the resemblance. Others say that as imitator and imitated both inhabit the same district, they are necessarily exposed to the same external conditions, producing the same amount of form and colour. This also is a perfectly untenable argument. It cannot be imagined that an insect resembles a green leaf or the bark of a tree, because both are exposed to the same physical conditions. By the Darwinian Theory of Natural Selection, the explanation of these remarkable analogies is sufficiently easy. All animals, without exception, are liable to variation in form, colour, and in size. Among insects in particular, variations of marking and form are most frequent. Let us now imagine a race of insects like those of the genus Leptalis, that have no special means of defence, and are consequently liable to be devoured by predaceous animals. When a variety of Leptalis arose which happened to resemble in any slight degree the offensive Heliconidæ, it would be much less liable to be pursued by predaceous animals than the unchanged original to which they were accustomed, hence that variety would have a greater chance of being propagated. Similar variations would occur in subsequent generations, those imitations that most closely resemble the model always being left, until at last this remarkable result would follow, that two insects, belonging to distinct families, would so closely resemble one another as only to be distinguished by a close inspection of their structural peculiarities."

INSECT DISGUISES.

A LARGE number of the members of the animal creation, especially of the world of insects, wear disguises, the study of which is most interesting on account of its very close bearing upon their history. In all cases of disguise it will be found to be of vital importance to the insect; and that portion of its structure which is concealed by the disguise often presents a striking contrast to the rest. Our common white butterflies are familiar but good examples, their colouring being so arranged that not a particle of the very conspicuous white is exposed when they are asleep, but only the dusky yellowish which colours the under sides of the hind wings and the tips of the fore wings. It may be further observed that this yellowish colour alone is visible only when the creature rests strictly speaking, and not when it merely settles on a leaf or flower on a sunny day—for the wings are then more or less open, and the white shows strongly; but in this case the insect is always thoroughly on the alert, and would avoid any approaching enemy by flight, while in the evening, or on very dull days, they are fast asleep, and, when found, as easy to capture as the plucking of the flower which they resemble. Their disguise is also aided by the fastidious care which they may be observed to use, as evening approaches, in choosing their sleeping-places, as they often change their places many times before settling down for the night.

The *Anthocharis cardamines*, or orange-tip, so beautiful as it gaily flutters along the hedgerows on a sunny spring morning, is most wonderfully protected by the colouring of its under surface when it is resting at night on the buds or blossoms of the *Anthriscus sylvestris*, or wild parsley, or some other small white flower, as shown in our coloured plate.

Mr. T. W. Wood says: "I have never seen the insect touch the wild parsley for any purpose but sleep, as it visits the little pink geranium, during sunshine, for the nectar it contains, at which time the wings are open, although not widely expanded. If the collector requires a few very fresh and uninjured specimens of this insect, he need only furnish himself with a few boxes, and walking along the hedgerows on a calm evening in May, his eyes will be gladdened by the pretty white bunches of wild parsley-blossom in great profusion, amongst which, and simulating them exactly, he will be sure either to spy or pass by the orange-tip. In the former case, all that is necessary is to open a box and close it very gently upon butterfly and flower, severing the flower stem outside the box, and placing it with its contents in his pocket. On arriving home, he will generally find that the insect has not moved in the least. Care should, however, be taken that the box is carried steadily, and that only a small piece of the blossom is enclosed, otherwise it may occupy too much room in the box, and the butterfly will be damaged in consequence. If carefully managed, the insect will not have been touched, and may now be killed without touching it, by placing the box under a tumbler with a few drops of Scheele's prussic acid on blotting paper, and in a very few moments the beautiful creature will be found lying dead and stiff at the bottom of the box; but it will be sure to relax the next day, and will then be fit for setting. This mode of capture I would recommend as being preferable in many respects to the one usually adopted with butterflies. There is no fluttering, and consequent damage, while in the net; the collector will not have to endanger his limbs by running madly over sometimes very uneven ground, with eye necessarily fixed only upon the one object of pursuit, which, when caught in the net, has to be disabled by a pinch in the thorax, intended to kill, which it never does; but the beauty and symmetry of form are often irretrievably injured by fracture of the outer skin or shell, which in all insects is their chief framework; legs are frequently broken off, and much beautiful down removed. By my plan all these drawbacks are avoided." The blue butterflies may be found in the evening, resting with their heads downwards on the buds and blossoms of grass, plantain, &c., which with their beautifully-spotted undersides and general appearance when in the attitude shown in our plate, they so closely resemble that they usually escape notice.

The chrysalides of butterflies possess a most extraordinary means of disguising themselves, their shells being photographically sensitive for a short time after the caterpillars' skins have been shed; so that each individual assumes the colour most prevalent in its immediate neighbourhood. As caterpillars are evidently unaffected by colour in their choice of a resting-place on which to undergo their transformations, this photographic power in the chrysalides is most important for their concealment during their period of exposure in a state of utter helplessness, which varies from a few weeks to half a year, and in some exceptional cases occupies more than a year.

The *Phlogophora meticulosa*, or angle-shades moth, shown in our coloured plate, is remarkable from its peculiar and probably unique appearance during the day, its time of resting, the fore wings being curled on their outer margins, thus adding greatly to the disguise, which is evidently that of a withered, dried-up leaf. The curl disappears immediately when the moth prepares for flight, and the wings then become as flat as those of any other insect.

There is a small moth belonging to the genus Antithesia, very common in gardens, shown on the central leaf in our coloured plate, which, when at rest, is exactly like the excrement of a sparrow, or other small bird, and, as we always find, the disguise it wears suits its habits, for it sits fully exposed to view on the upper surface of leaves, &c., and will drop off when the leaves are shaken as if it were really a lifeless object.

A most beautiful example of disguise among caterpillars is found in that of the *Papilio machaon*, or swallow-tailed butterfly, which feeds on carrot leaves. The black markings of the insect, as viewed from the side, closely imitate the interstices between the smaller serrated leaflets; the diagonal terminations of the stripes on each side greatly aid the resemblance, and even the orange spots are placed exactly where that colour begins to appear on the carrot leaf, namely, at the points of the serrations; while in size also the insect and its markings agree exactly with the leaves. (*See Engraving.*)

These few examples will doubtless excite the reader's interest; but there is a vast field for observation, and if he will search carefully in our gardens, heaths, and woods, he will find many and extraordinary forms of insect disguises which will amply repay the time and labour he may devote to this interesting subject.

1
3
W. H. Fitch.

THE OAK-FEEDING SILKWORM OF CHINA.

CHINA was undoubtedly the country in which men first availed themselves of the labours of the silkworm. Aristotle is the first Greek author who mentions the silkworm (Nat. Hist. V. 19); and he states that silk was first spun in the island of Cos, but the raw material was still an oriental product. For many centuries it was not known in Europe from what source silk was produced. It was not indeed until the sixth century that the obscurity which enveloped this subject was cleared up by the successful result of a journey, made by two Nestorian monks, to China to unravel the mystery. The breeding of silkworms in Europe was for six centuries confined to the Greeks of the Lower Empire. In the twelfth century the art was transferred to Sicily; in the thirteenth century the rearing of silkworms and the manufacture of silk were introduced into Italy, whence it was successively introduced into Spain and France, and in the fifteenth century the manufacture was established in England.

One of the most interesting of the silkworm family is the *Bombyx mori*, well known as the moth to which the silkworm turns. This species, which was originally from China, is of a white or cream colour, with a brown fascia and two or more waved lines of a deeper colour crossing the upper wings. In this country the eggs of this moth are hatched early in May. The caterpillar, or silkworm, is at first of a dark colour, but soon becomes light, and in its tints much resembles the perfect insect—a circumstance common in caterpillars. Its proper food is the mulberry, though it will likewise eat the lettuce and some few other plants; on these plants, however, it does not thrive equally well, and the silk yielded is of a poor quality.

The disease which made such ravages amongst the *Bombyx mori*, or common silkworm, in the South of Europe, caused attention to be directed to new sources for supply, or at least for additions to the ordinary supply of silk, which, like the cotton, paper, and cinchona supply, had become a question of the greatest importance. In the great silk-cultivating districts in the South of Europe, a failure or deficiency in the supply of that commodity would cause great poverty among the people of those countries, and as much distress among our silk-weavers as the want of cotton inflicted upon our Lancashire operatives. Science has also gained something, and will probably gain more, from the experiments in the acclimatisation of various species, as in the case of the *Bombyx Cynthia*, or ailanthus worm, which has been proved not only to exist, but even to be more healthy and vigorous, in this country than in France. It is now about fourteen years since the *Bombyx Cynthia* was first reared in Europe, and since then many other species from India, China, Japan, and Australia have been brought into notice.

The latest of these is the oak-feeding silkworm of China, or *Antherœa Pernyi*. It produces what is known as mountain silk, which has of late become a most important article of trade amongst the Chinese. Specimens of the foliage and the acorns of the oaks upon which they feed, together with some cocoons containing some chrysalids, and some hanks of the silk, were received at Kew from China about four years ago, and from these specimens the species of oaks were ascertained. Mr. Jackson, the Curator of the Museum at the Royal Gardens, Kew, says: "Two of them, called by the Chinese respectively large and small 'Tsing-kang-lew,' appear to be *Quercus Mongolica*. Another called 'Hoo-pŏ-lŏ' is *Quercus obovata*, Bunge, the leaves of which are larger and darker in colour than those of *Quercus Mongolica*. There is also a marked difference in the acorns, which are larger, and the scales long and tapering, and of a dark brown colour, thus giving to the cup the appearance of being covered with long brown fur, which also partly covers the acorn itself. The fourth is "Tseen-tso-tsze," and is the *Quercus serrata* of Thunberg. The silkworms fed upon this oak produce the best silk; the tree, however, is not so common in the silk districts as either of the other species. The next best quality of silk is produced by feeding the insects upon the leaves of *Quercus Mongolica*, those of *Quercus obovata* producing the most inferior description. Two crops of silk are produced by the *Antheræa Pernyi* in one year—a spring and an autumn crop. The cocoons, which are very large, are carefully selected by the silk growers after the autumn crop of silk has been collected, and stored away in baskets, which are usually hung up in ordinary living rooms for the spring. The ordinary heat of a Chinese living room during the winter seems to be quite sufficient to prevent the frost affecting the chrysalids. The temperature of a Chinese dwelling in the mountain silk districts is during the greater part of the winter considerably below freezing-point. It is thought that the chrysalis would not be affected even if exposed on the trees during an ordinary winter night in the Chinese forests, and if this be so, it will probably prove hardy enough to bear our climate. Towards the end of April the oaks upon which the caterpillars feed begin to open their young leaves; and to push forward the growth of these leaves, so as to have food in readiness for the caterpillars when hatched, twigs are cut off the trees, and placed either in tubs of water in dwelling-houses, or in pools and mountain streams. By the time the leaves have expanded, the moths have made their escape from the cocoons, have paired, deposited their eggs, which are hatched on sheets of paper upon which the young leaves of the oak are placed. The insects are thus nursed and nourished for a few days, by which time they have grown to about an inch in length. They are then transferred to the trees themselves on the hill slopes, the younger and most tender-leaved plants being selected. Some days elapse before the caterpillar moults for the first time; it also changes its colour from black to green, and increases considerably in size. It goes through four of these changes, after each of which its bulk is increased, but it retains its green colour. It now begins spinning its silk, and of course encloses itself in its cocoon, there again to take the chrysalis form. These natural changes are gone through much quicker in the spring than in the autumn season, a difference of five or six weeks existing. In each season, as fast as the caterpillars consume the leaves of one oak bush they are removed by the attendant silk cultivator to another, the youngest bushes being first used."

Mr. Meadows, the English Consul at Newchang, says: "Just before spinning its cocoon, it is a bright green-bodied grub or caterpillar, of about 3½ to 4 inches in length, with a light brown head. On its pale brown face there are six or eight small black specks. Its body has twelve joints. When the worm begins to make its cocoon, it selects two or more oak leaves, more or less facing each other, and lower than the twig from which they proceed. These leaves it joins together by a network of its silk thread, which thread keeps issuing from its mouth as it moves its head from one leaf to the other. It holds on, in the meantime, by its back claws to the twig. When the leaves are sufficiently joined to form a sort of cup or basket under the twig to which it is holding, it loosens its hold, and drops into the receptacle it has thus formed. The hindermost seven joints of the body are then with the tail joints slightly curled in, drawn together, and, remaining in a state of total inaction, serve, I presume, merely as a store from which the silk thread matter is drawn. The work of further self-enclosure the animal does with his head, and the foremost five joints of the body. It first quite surrounds itself with the loose flossy-like silk which forms the outer portion of the cocoons as they come to market, and through which its green body remains for a time visible. It then gradually forms the dense, hardish, skin-like substance which constitutes the inner portion of the cocoon. On opening a cocoon which had been recently formed, and was to outward appearance quite finished, I found inside a complete green worm curled up in the way I have described as to its hind part, and with the fore part in the condition in which it is when the animal is in one of its sleeps on the bush. After a while the fore part began to move, and the animal to spin silk, which it attached at each turn of its head to the surface of a table on which I had placed it. It seemed to be labouring to increase the thickness of its cocoon, being, doubtless, roused to the necessity of so doing by the feel of the open air to which it was again exposed. I judged that if the cocoon had not been opened, the animal would, after a sleep in it, have proceeded to thicken the inner surface by further thread-spinning, and have gone on so doing till its bulk was sufficiently decreased for its turning into the chrysalis shape."

From this description of the *Atheræa Pernyi*, or oak-feeding silkworm, it will be seen that it very closely agrees in habits with the *Bombyx Cynthia*, or ailanthus-feeder; and if it should succeed in our climate as well as that insect, and feed upon the leaves of any of our British oaks, it will be a valuable acquisition. The silk appears very strong, and, properly cleaned, would, doubtless, be sufficiently bright and flossy, and will probably make an important import from China.

These insects are not only useful as silk producers in their native country, but their huge bodies are drawn out by the Chinese into fishing-lines, which are of a somewhat similar nature to catgut. We are told by a celebrated traveller in China that these can sometimes be drawn out to a continuous length of fifteen or twenty yards.*

Fig. 1 in the plate represents the cocoon, natural size; Fig. 2, the chrysalis, natural size; Fig. 3, the moth, natural size. The leaves and acorn are those of *Quercus serrata*, of Thunberg, which produce the best kind of silk.

---

* For the process of making silkworm gut, see "Sea Fishing as a Sport," by L. J. H. Young. Price 5s. Groombridge & Sons, 5, Paternoster Row, London.

INSECTS' EGGS.

NEARLY all insects are oviparous, or produce their young by eggs. In form, colour, character, and beauty of design, the eggs of insects are more surprisingly varied than those of the feathered tribes. The elaboration of structure and variety of forms in a large number might be turned to a practical account, as many suggest patterns of great beauty and delicacy for art designs. Our knowledge of the composition of either the exterior or interior is not so complete as in the case of birds' eggs. Those of our readers who may wish for information on the structure should read an able article on the subject by Mr. Jabez Hogg, which appeared in the *Intellectual Observer* for December, 1867.

The eggs of moths and butterflies present many varying tints of colour, the prevailing being yellow, white, grey, and a light brown. In some eggs the yellow, white, and grey are delicately blended; and these, when viewed with a magnifying power of about fifty diameters, and by the aid of a side reflector (parabolic reflector), present many beautiful combinations, and the most delicate opalescent, or rather iridescent tints appear on others.

The egg of the *Abraxas grossularia*, or Magpie moth (Fig. 1), is very delicate and silvery in tone, and the membrane is so translucent that the movements of the young worm within can be very well seen. The egg of the *Aspilates gilvaria*, or Straw-belle moth (Fig. 2), is very delicately tinted; it is somewhat long and narrow in form, with sides slightly flattened or rounded off, and is regularly serrated. The top is convex, and the base a little indented. The *Exarnis ypsilon*, or Dingy shears (Fig. 3), lays a small sub-conical egg,

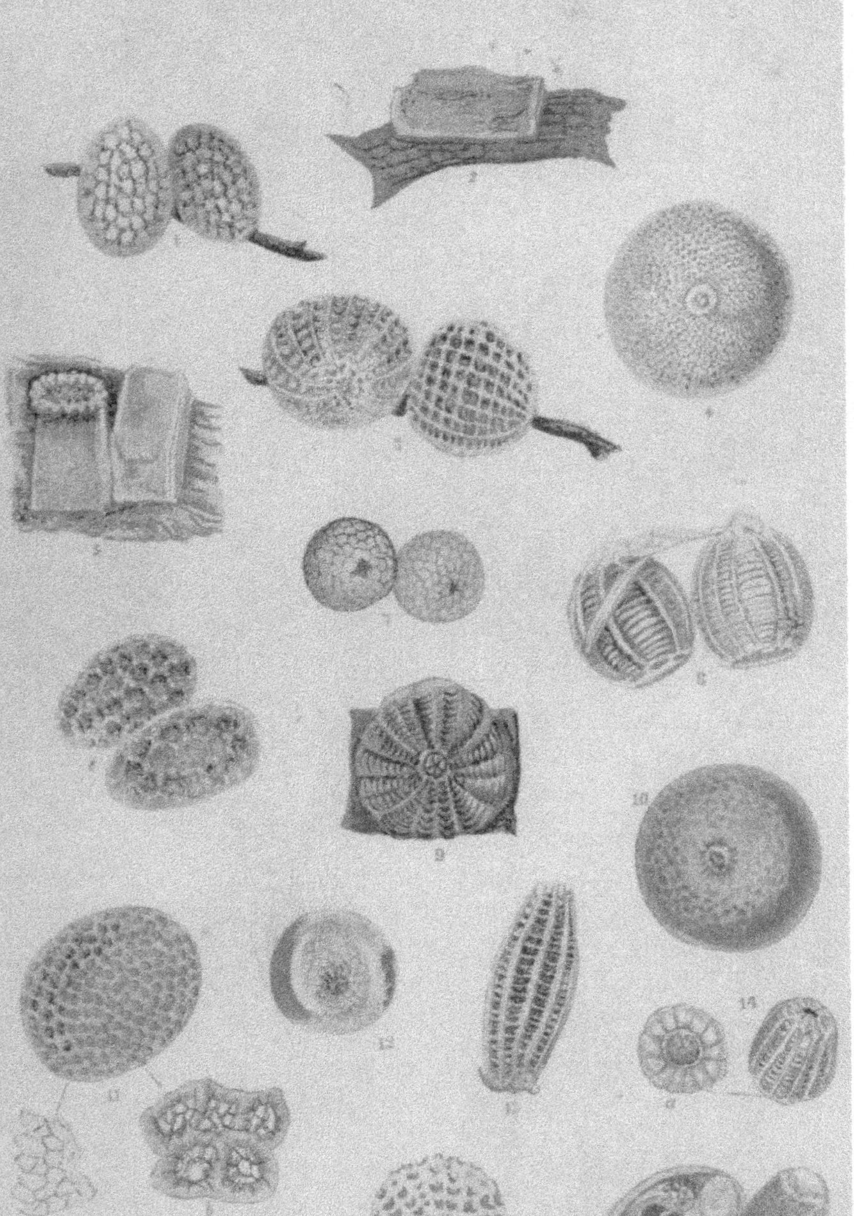

W. F. Maples, del.

INSECT EGGS.

with a flattened base, which admits of its being firmly cemented to either bark or leaf. The egg is beautifully reticulated, the ribs are slightly raised from the membrane, and connected with each other by cross-bars; they run from a marginal ring in regular order to the base, and a series of fine lines radiates from the central spot to the border. The egg of the *Pheosia dictæa*, or Swallow-prominent (Fig. 4), is spheroidal, slightly flattened at the poles, and, with the exception of one spot, the surface is a continued series of regular indentations, reminding one of those fine reticulations, or markings, seen on some of the Guiano shells. The colour is a very delicate pink. That of the *Ennomos erosaria*, or Thorn moth (Fig. 5), is of an elongated square form, one end of which is slightly tapered off, while the other is flattened. The empty eggshell gives a fine opalescent play of colours, while that containing the young worm appears of a brownish yellow colour. The *Diacrisia russula*, or Buff-tiger moth (Fig. 7), lays an exquisite little globular egg, the external membrane of which is covered by a fine network of irregular hexagons. It has all the appearance of an iridescent minute glass globule, and is so translucent that the young worm can be seen through it. The egg of the *Erannis defoliaria*, or Mottled-umber moth (Fig. 8), is in every particular very beautiful. It is ovoid, with regular hexagonal reticulations, each corner being studded with a white raised knob or button. The space within the hexagon is finely punctuated; and the play of colours is exquisitely delicate. That of the *Hylophila prasinana*, or small Silver-lines moth (Fig. 9), is yellow brown, in form a truncated pyramid. A series of raised ribs are set in regular order around the sides, and the cross-bars, which connect them, presenting a pretty basket-like pattern. The egg is flattened out at the base, apparently for the purpose of securing it more firmly to the leaf. The *Cerura vinula* or Puss moth (Fig. 10), lays a large spheroidal shaped egg, having, under the microscope, the appearance of a fine ripe orange. The surface of the egg is finely reticulated, or rather has the appearance of a piece of netting stretched tightly over it. The colour is a deep orange. A remarkable instance of the change of colour, which occurs from physiological causes connected with the development of the embryo, and one from which the insect partly derives its name, is seen in the *Endromus versicolor*, or Glory of Kent. The egg is first bright yellow, then successively green, rose colour, and reddish black. A still more familiar instance is presented in the egg of the *Bombyx mori*, or Silkworm moth (Fig. 11), which, when first laid, is of a delicate pale yellow; this hue it retains for some time; it is subsequently of a reddish brown, and just before the embryo quits the egg it acquires a slate colour, partaking for the time being of the colour of the embryo within; but so soon as the worm emerges forth, the shell regains its original pale yellow. The outer and inner portions of the egg membrane are represented magnified 150 diameters at *a* and *b* (Fig. 11). The *Euproctis chrysorrhœa*, or Browntail moth (Fig. 12), produces a small spheroidal egg, which, slightly flattened at the poles, is uniformly covered with imbricated scales, and is terminated in the upper pole by a geometrical series; this moth appears to cover her eggs with fine hairs, and the empty spherical egg-cases are beautifully iridescent. The *Pieris brassicæ*, or White butterfly (Fig. 13), lays an egg in shape very like the basket employed in lobster-fishing, a rarer form than any of the preceding. It is conical, and of considerable length; the lid forms the base, which is slightly recurved upon the sides, and a regular series of ribs with cross-bars runs from end to end. The eggs are of a primrose colour and cemented at the base to the back or leaf of the plant in symmetrical order. The *Epinephile janira*, or Meadow-brown butterfly (Fig. 14), lays a sub-conical egg, considerably flattened towards the apex; the raised ribs, which stand away from the sides, have a silvery colour, and give to the whole a corrugated appearance. The lid completely occupies the top, and in a smaller inner circle the micropyle is situated, which is better displayed when the lid is separated from the egg, as shown at *a*. The *Thecla betulæ*, or Brown-hair streak butterfly (Fig. 15) presents a perfectly white, exquisitely formed, sub-conical egg; at first sight it might be compared to a beautiful ivory-turned ball in miniature. It is covered by a series of deep indentations or pits, with regularly projecting spines. The egg of the *Jodis vernaria*, or small Emerald Volute moth (Fig. 16), is remarkable in form, which is somewhat oval, but flattened on the broad side, of silvery whiteness, covered with minute reticulations and dots, peculiarly translucent, so much so that the little yellow-brown worm is seen curled up within, as shown in the egg to the left. Fig. 17 is the egg of the Honey-bee, showing the germinal vesicle.

THE MICROSCOPE.

The invention of the microscope has opened a new world to us. "It has been well observed," says Professor Whewell, "that about the same time when the invention of the telescope showed us that there might be myriads of other worlds claiming the Creator's care, the invention of the microscope proved to us that there were in our own world myriads of creatures, before unknown, which this care was preserving. While one discovery seemed to remove the Divine Providence further from us, the other gave us more striking examples that it was far more active in our neighbourhood than we had supposed; while the first extended the boundaries of God's known kingdom, the second made its known administration more minute and careful.

"It appeared that in the leaf, and in the bud, in solids and fluids, animals existed hitherto unsuspected; the apparently dead masses and blank spaces of the world were found to swarm with life. And yet, of the animals thus revealed, all, though unknown to us before, had never been forgotten by Providence. Their structure, their vessels and limbs, their adaptation to the situation, their food and habitations, were regulated in as beautiful and complete a manner as those of the largest and apparently most favoured animals. The smallest insects are as exactly finished, often as gaily ornamented, as the most graceful beasts, or birds of the brightest plumage. And when we seem to go out of the domain of the complex animal structure with which we are familiar, and come to animals of apparently more scanty faculties and less developed powers of enjoyment and action, we still find that their faculties and their senses are in exact harmony with their situation and circumstances; that the wants which they have are provided for, and the powers which they possess called into action. We find, therefore, that Divine Providence is, in fact, extended over an immense succession of tribes of beings, surpassing what we could have conceived or expected; and thus we may feel secure that the mere multitude of created objects cannot remove us from the government and superintendence of our Creator."

Upon examining the edge of a very keen razor with a microscope, it will appear as broad as the back of a thick knife: rough, uneven, full of notches and furrows. An exceedingly small needle resembles a rough iron bar. But the sting of a bee, seen through the same instrument, exhibits everywhere a polish most amazingly beautiful, without the least flaw, blemish, or inequality, and it ends in a point too fine to be discerned. A small piece of exceedingly fine lawn appears, through a microscope, like a hurdle or lattice, and the threads themselves seem coarser than the yarn with which ropes are made for anchors. But a silkworm's web appears perfectly smooth and shining, and everywhere equal. The smallest dot that can be made with a pen, appears, when viewed by the microscope, an irregular spot, rough, jagged, and uneven. But the little specks on the wings or bodies of insects are found to be most accurately circular. The finest miniature paintings appear before this instrument as mere daubings, plastered on with a trowel, entirely void of beauty, either in the drawing or the colouring. The most even and beautiful varnishes and polishings will be found to be mere roughness, full of gaps and flaws. Thus sink the works of art before the microscopic eye. But the nearer we examine the works of God, even in the least of His productions, the more sensible shall we be of His wisdom and power. Apply the microscope to any, the most minute, of His works, nothing is to be found but beauty and perfection. If we examine the numberless species of insects that swim, creep, or fly around us, what proportion, exactness, uniformity, and symmetry, shall we perceive in all their organs! what a profusion of colouring!—azure, green, and vermilion, gold, silver, pearls, rubies, and diamonds; fringe and embroidery on their bodies, wings, heads, and every other part! How high the finishing! how inimitable the polish we everywhere behold! The most perfect works of man betray a meanness, a poverty, an inability in the workman; but the works of nature plainly prove that

"The hand that made them is Divine."

CPSIA information can be obtained
at www.ICGtesting.com
Printed in the USA
LVHW100613210323
742065LV00002B/289

9 783382 126315